KAIJU CHRYSALIS

SAM M. PHILLIPS

SEVEREDPRESS

KAIJU CHRYSALIS

Copyright © 2025 Sam M. Phillips

WWW.SEVEREDPRESS.COM

ISBN: 978-1-923165-80-9

1

The sky was on fire.

It was a canvas of chaos, crisscrossed with screaming fighter jets and diving bombers. They trailed in dizzying spirals and swooping arcs through dazzling explosions. Red and yellow flames scoured the blue firmament as missiles struck home, planes snatched from the air as if by an angry, crushing fist. In their wake the puffs of black smoke were like mottled bruises which faded fast but were quickly replaced in a cycle of violence and abuse, pawns traded for pawns, with nothing gained.

This was a cataclysm, a war where all hope was lost, victory out of reach for all.

Faceless pilots died in their masses, their stories untold except in statistics, mourned only by invisible families far away, whose pain awaited them sometime in the future. Unknown to them, a sword was hanging over their as yet everyday existence, soon to drop and cleave them in two, one part dying with their loved one, the other continuing on, haunting life in a hollowed out existence.

For those still living in this orgy of death there was only adrenaline and nerve-shredding strain, the pace fast as the planes blasted away with their weapons, torturing the sky further with a million spent bullets. These traced lines like a spray of laser beams in a lightshow, their colours and shapes kaleidoscopic, almost beautiful in their mesmerising display.

But they were the patterns which accompanied mass murder. These were the words of agony wrought like skywriting across what had once been an idyllic vista of white clouds against a cool blue background. The fiery explosions were the punctuation marks, ending life sentences of those condemned to serve in the military.

The killing was without mercy, the slaughter continuous.

What was being witnessed was a world inverted, where the heavens had become a fiery hell. The ground below was purgatory, filled with helpless onlookers, necks craning up to watch. They anticipated their inevitable fates, handed out like playing cards in a game of chance as pieces of war debris rained like hail. A man's head was sliced through with a falling chunk of a wing, a baby killed by unexploded ordinance which crushed its tiny body like a dropped rock. Fleeing meant nothing, for the rain of destruction was everywhere, the bombers looming over their marks, disgorging their payloads.

This was not life. It was waiting for death.

Even further down though, beneath the surface, was a subterranean peace, the world of worms and microscopic bugs. They burrowed through their tranquil existence, far removed from the chaos of man, machine, and monster far above, yet feasting on the corpses supplied in abundance from that realm. Theirs was the real paradise, and if there was pain, there were at least no thoughts of it to afflict these simple creatures. They ate what remained of the suffering which trickled down to them, blissfully content and unknowing of the awful, horrifying truth— that the final death had come, the end of the world.

But this world wasn't Earth. It was a faraway planet, one invented in the mind, committed to paper in a creative frenzy, bound up in a book with colourful and fantastical cover art. A young woman sat in a chair on a porch, reading about that planet. She was enraptured by its trials and tribulations, its politics and conflicts, the lives of its inhabitants vivid and visceral. As if by some type of infectious transference of ideas, the words of the author passed from their mind to hers, communicated in magical symbols of black ink printed on creamy white paper. It didn't matter that the author was long dead. They lived on in the mind of the woman as she read. Neither did it matter that everything she imagined in her mind was made up. For her, the battle of high-tech planes, and everything else in that science fiction story, was real and dreadfully important. They allowed her a means to escape.

Not that her own reality, sipping coffee and reading on that porch in a little village on the planet Earth, was so awful. But it soon would be. Something monstrous was coming. And when it arrived there would be no escape.

2

Breanne put down the now empty coffee cup, but she couldn't put down the book. She needed to know how things turned out for both sides in their cosmically vast galactic war. But as she reached the end of the story, she realised there was no real resolution to the conflict. Instead an infuriatingly enticing cliff-hanger left things open-ended for a sequel.

"Damn, they've already done, what, eight books?" she said. "I guess it's meant to be a trilogy of trilogies, but come on, what the hell happens already?" She tossed the book down in disgust. "If I ever write a book, I'm going to make sure there's a good ending for every book, not some click bait so I have to buy the next one."

She sighed, shoulders slumping.

But you're never going to write a book, are you?

"Shut up," she said back at her thoughts, getting up from her chair defiantly. "I'm not letting my dyslexia get the better of me."

But she didn't need dyslexia to stop her from starting the long-promised project of a story of her own, something to match those she idolised. Her ADHD did a good enough job of that by itself. As it was though, the two dysfunctions could tag-team her all day, meaning she was lucky to even *read* a book.

Let alone do all the planning, and thinking, and world building... and then writing, and editing, and...

"Okay, you win this round, but tomorrow, I'm going to make a start, and that's a promise," she said, going through the same old routine she always did to trick herself.

But while she was busy procrastinating some things—those she considered most important precisely because they weren't getting done—she did plenty of other things. And though she bounced around between these like crazy, they added up to something which resembled a productive life. After reading, she did the dishes and a load of laundry. Then she searched for more dishes and laundry to do, because these types of tasks always felt satisfying to complete—short, fast, doable.

Painting wasn't so easy, and while she sat down in front of the canvas, momentarily inspired by the visions the book had placed in her mind, she couldn't bring herself to squeeze any paint onto her palette, or even to get the graphite pencil, start sketching in the shapes of the dogfighting planes amidst fiery explosions.

She frowned, eyes squeezed shut, but the vision faded so quickly it felt impossible she'd ever be able to capture it. Looking around the garage—her makeshift studio while her parents were away on deployment—all she saw were half-finished pieces, and the visions that had inspired *them* were now so long gone they had no hope of ever being finished.

If only I could take a picture of what I see in my mind when I'm reading. If only my daydreams could be captured in situ. Then I'd be a real artist.

"Even if you finish a painting, you'll not have written a book," she said, giving herself a kick while she was down that she didn't need. "Maybe I need a walk to clear my head."

Then you'll come back with a nice, peaceful, yet empty brain, with nothing to commit to the page or canvas.

"Ah, yes, but I'll have that peace you mentioned, and isn't that the point of completing anything? A moment where we say to ourselves that's enough, you're alright as you are, you can finally rest."

But you're not enough are you, because even if you had peace, or a book written, or a painting completed, you don't have a partner, do you? And why's that?

"Because I'm ugly," she said, and felt a perverse need to go look in a mirror to confirm this. She stopped in the hallway, halfway to her temporary bedroom—normally her parents'—with its full length dressing mirror, unwilling to continue. She didn't need reminding of her bad posture or mousey hair. She couldn't bring herself to peer through the thick glasses she wore to see her mediocre features and average body, always hidden beneath baggy clothes but always there, lurking beneath this thin veneer, ready to wreck her self-esteem on the jagged rocks of her unrealistic expectations.

She glanced at the women's magazine her mother had left on the stand in the hall.

"Damn it, Mum, you're in the Navy. Why the hell don't you have Guns and Ammo or some shit like that, rather than these?"

She scowled angrily at the magazines. It wasn't her place to throw them out—Breanne was house sitting after all—but she could open a drawer, put them away. Something prevented her from doing this, as if she were preserving the place as closely as possible to the way her parents had left it, like a shrine. This felt wrong to do, as if she was accepting they might not come back.

"The war's in your head, not out there," she told herself. "Don't let that book convince you they're in danger."

Authors fuck with our emotions so much, she thought. *For once I want to be the one to fuck, instead of being fucked by them.*

She laughed in a single exclamation, a sharp exhale of air, and said, "You're not getting fucked by anyone."

Breanne looked wistfully at the beautiful woman on the cover of the magazine.

If only…

The thought trailed off, unfinished, and she let it die on the vine. Instead, she looked up at the pictures of her parents hung in the hallway. There were lots of photos of the two of them together or individually, especially in their Australian Navy uniforms. In some they wore pressed dress whites and in others grey and black camouflage fatigues. Both showed a progression through the officer ranks over time as they aged, the insignia on their shoulders evolving into more elaborate shapes in gold stitching to accompany the expanding strings of medals and colourful ribbons on their chests.

There were fewer pictures of the whole family together and none of Breanne alone. In the couple in which she was present she looked like an ugly duckling in between a pair of elegant white swans. Where they were tall and proud, she was stooped and awkward, their clothes neat, reflecting internal discipline, her clothes were… well, her clothes were symbolic of the chaos which seemed to surround her everywhere.

Everywhere but here, she thought, referring to the house, the village. She went out the back door. She surveyed the orderly gardens with their neat beds of flowers and plants, oases of woodchips in an expanse of clipped, green grass.

It's beautiful. If only I was like my parents I could make a life this beautiful for myself. I could be this perfect. But no, I'm the fuck up. I'm surprised they even let me watch the house while they're away.

She went over to the tap, turned it on, activating the sprinklers. They sprang into life, glistening jets of water streaming across the precious garden.

"At least I'm good for something," she said and went back inside.

3

"Don't drink another cup of coffee," she told herself as she paced the house, looking for something to do.

It'll make you more productive, her thoughts told her. She knew this was a lie. The day was ending and she was still too hyper. In spite of this she hadn't achieved what she'd hoped to achieve. The illusion that more coffee would help her now was just that, an illusion.

"All it will do is keep you up all night," she said, but she was already mechanically going through the motions, unable to resist the lure of her parents' expensive coffee machine.

"After all, it's free, right?"

No, nothing is free. Think of what it's going to cost you.

The coffee was already made. She sipped it appreciatively as the afternoon waned into early evening. She looked out the window, meditatively watching the swaying cane fields down in the valley. She thought of every meal she'd ever eaten in this house when visiting, back home from university. With criticisms disguised as jokes, her father had made her feel like she owed him yard work for everything she ate in his house, for every night she slept in one of his beds. It was a debt she could never work off. Same as the calories she consumed were a body debt she could never get ahead of.

She walked to the pantry. It was well-stocked with food Breanne's mother had left for her.

This food is like payment for the housesitting, so why don't I eat any of it?

She picked up a packet, read the ingredients and the serving size information. Her stomach growled like a hungry beast, angry at her for giving it nothing but

8

coffee all day. She placed the packet back on the shelf and put her shoes on as mechanically as she'd made the coffee. There was no thought process, everything done on instinct, ingrained patterns of self-abuse, the judgements from others she'd internalised.

Her parents were so fit. They were in the defence forces. They were disciplined and worked out constantly. They watched what they ate.

Dad eats too much sugar, though.

Breanne looked at her hand. There was a half-eaten chocolate bar in it.

"The fuck…?" she said, dropping it on the kitchen bench like it was covered in cockroaches. The repugnance couldn't overpower the habit though, some dopamine driven manic puppeteer inside her immediately snatching it up again and wolfing it down greedily.

She was out the front door before she could think, her shoes tapping an anxiety-ridden staccato across the porch and down the stairs. She crunched along the gravel path between the neat, all-too-perfect flowerbeds, goaded by an internal demon. It jabbed at the base of her brain with a red hot poker, the reptilian centre there snarling like an enraged monster.

She would no longer be taking the peaceful walk she planned earlier. Now it was about paying off the debt.

4

Breanne was about four streets into the walk before she slowed down a bit from her aggressive pace, the coffee and sugar finally wearing off. With these factors removed, the blinkers came off her tunnel vision and she could look around, side to side, and take in her surroundings. There were pleasant yet dated houses on generous blocks of land, lawns neatly tended, big trees with lazy branches hanging over the streets, the birds singing their last as the light of the fading sun turned red then purple.

She managed a smile. The village was a nice place. She enjoyed coming back here, for all the triggering it did even without the active voice of her parents' physical presence. Growing up here had had its challenges, not the least of which was that it was isolating. For all their friendliness, the neighbours kept to themselves, or perhaps Breanne kept to herself, and she'd never made any actual friends here. It didn't help that this was an ageing community, not ideal for an active social life as a teen, nor now she'd turned twenty.

It was a stark contrast to everything she experienced living in a share-house down the road from the university she attended, but that was in the city. There people were packed in and she was forced to commingle. Here in the country she had only herself and her vicious cycle of self-deprecating thoughts, ones originally born in this seemingly idyllic environment.

She reached the end of a street, one which terminated down the bottom of the big hill on which the village sat. Here the sugarcane fields came right up to the road, separated only by an irrigation-cum-firebreak ditch filled with swampy water. Looking at the tall stalks of sugarcane, it was easy to get nostalgic for the cane cutting season, when they'd first burn off the chaff with controlled fires. The whole field would go up in a massive inferno, a vision of hell on Earth, eerily beautiful, strange and mesmerising. It was an act of destruction which created something, the cane harvested for sugar—

Please don't mention sugar.

—by massive tractor machines and then a rotation crop like soybean planted to put nitrogen back into the tired soil. They didn't grow those soybeans for food, just ploughed them back into the dirt, ready to plant the sugar cash crop again.

It was an endless cycle culminating in the climax of the hypnotic, consuming fire which had captured mankind's imagination since the dawn of time. It was like some ritual sacrifice, the burning of bodies so new life could spring forth.

But then fell the inevitable ash from the cane fires, filling the sky like an ominous cloud and raining down like tainted snow. Covering everything in soot, it was the black cape of the Grim Reaper, reminding everyone that the big farming corporations didn't care a damn about the environment or the residents of the village. It covered her parents' precious flowers, stained them dark. It polluted the village and gave people headaches. It soiled their perfect environment, the one all the residents here thought was isolated—in the best possible way— from the problems of the wider world.

But Breanne knew better. Years of reading books and watching documentaries taught her there was always something evil out there, keen to burst forth from the shadows and destroy that which basked in the sunshine. It was chaos, a force of nature to balance against order in an endless battle. Like the growth and reaping of the sugarcane, their dance was a lifecycle. They were two sides of the same process, with a fiery conflict marking the transition from one to the other, everything nearby getting burned in the process.

The site of this eternal war between light and darkness shifted across the world, blighting one community after another. All anyone could do was move away, shift themselves out of the path of the falling ash.

But is anywhere safe? It's all an illusion, a story we tell ourselves so we can sleep at night.

Breanne stared thoughtfully into the stagnant water of the irrigation ditch. There were tiny ripples in the water, as if something large was disturbing the surface, though still far away. She felt its looming presence, saw the impact anything large enough could have even at a distance. The conclusion was inevitable—nowhere was safe on this Earth.

As if to prove her point, the mosquitoes—triggered by her presence and the approach of dusk—rose up from their birthing pools in the ditch. They swarmed her in a vicious buzzing pack, proboscises stabbing like tiny knives into exposed flesh. Breanne's anxiety spiked once more as she was forced to flee up the hill, back towards the village, back home, her arms flailing, like this would do anything to fend off those thousands of hungry mouths which sought to prey upon her, suck her blood.

Nowhere is safe.

5

Breanne had one safe space—the internet. There she felt capable of being herself—or someone else, if it suited her mood—though it was possible both her actual and fake profiles on social media were as false as each other. With posts, photos, and comments she projected a happy image of her life, something she didn't feel, but her cyber personas lived by the adage 'fake it until you make it.'

She had few photos of herself on any of her own profiles, preferring to lead with cute puppy and kitten photos. Her parents' garden had been helpful with the amount of flower pictures she'd been able to take with her phone and post, though just as many were harvested from Google. The pictures she allowed of herself were in relation to various fandoms, at conventions wearing costumes, where others enjoyed her creativity and treated her—or the characters she represented, of which they were fans—with respect and inclusivity. These photos showed a true part of her, one of the sides of herself which didn't feel oppressed by her looks or her differentness.

Though maybe I'm not so different from my folks, after all, she thought, sitting at her laptop, checking the number of likes on one of these photos. *They dress up in a costume, play a role. They want to be part of something bigger than themselves. Isn't that what we all want?*

"I'd settle for a single person to share this with," she said, sitting at the kitchen table and frowning at the low like-count on her post. It was more than a single like, but she mentally divided everything on social media by one hundred, so even if a few people liked and commented, it may as well be zero, or even negative.

Perhaps if I get famous and lots of people adore me, it will add up to the love I need... from my parents, from a partner, from anyone.

"But not from myself," she said out loud. She wasn't totally ignorant of her subconscious makeup, of the psychological forces which pressed upon her. But knowing didn't undo them, and perhaps ignorance was bliss, because she searched feverishly for a way to help herself, reading article after article online.

She also tried messaging girls. It always began with overtures of friendship, testing the waters, Breanne trying to discover herself along the way. But the chats, sometimes stretching over months, ended in failure as the other women either left her in the friend zone—and who could blame them?—or they freaked out when she tried to hint at something more, and left. The process was taking its toll on her, each defeat a further condemnation of her character, or of the character she'd invented, which was worse somehow. It made her reluctant to try again.

But try again she did, more desperate each time, and more inclined to lie and deceive in order to try to find the winning formula. Breanne didn't like the term 'catfish,' but she knew that's what she was, and through even these false fronts failing to attract much interest it slowly dawned on her that something must be wrong with her, for she was the common denominator between all these personas. The photos changed—stolen from ever-more beautiful strangers on Google—but the person in the chat didn't. Even when pretending to be someone else she was herself. Because she invented them they could only behave as seen through the lens of her own experience.

I can't even invent attractive people convincingly! No wonder I can't write a book. It might as well be called The Diary of a Loser, and there's no text, just a photo of me, taken from a bad angle so I look like I've got three chins.

All this made her hate herself and feel even more rejected and alone. She couldn't help but wish she'd been born different.

But no, I have to be Breanne, don't I? Who else would want to be me? Not even I want to be me. I'm not even good enough for a catfish. No one would pretend to be me, because what would be the point?

"Maybe for use in some type of credit card scam, I don't know."

You're not pretty enough to convince people to hand over their personal info, dumbass.

She sighed, refreshing her web browser, hoping some more likes would magically appear.

"If only I wasn't gay, then at least I'd have a chance," she said, thinking of her parents and their heteronormative relationship.

They're happy, aren't they?

Breanne's parents didn't know she was gay. She doubted they even cared.

Was that because they're in the Navy?

It was an inevitable question, though with an equally inevitable answer.

No, it's because they don't care about me, period.

Breanne got up from the table. Leaving the laptop behind in the kitchen she went into the hall. She grabbed the bundle of women's magazines from the stand, no longer concerned with what her parents thought, or with preserving the tokens of their precious orderly life. She brought them back into the kitchen, stomping on the bin's lever to open it. Poised to dump the magazines in the bin, she thought she was going to do it, but then she caught sight of the gorgeous women on the covers.

Removing her foot, the bin lid clinked closed. Driven by unconscious forces which collided with conscious reasoning, she took them into her parents' bedroom where she'd been sleeping, laid them out so she could view them all at once. The blank glossy eyes of the women stared back at her.

If I can't be them, at least I can be with *them,* she thought, reaching down the front of her jeans.

6

Breanne awoke with a start at the sound of torrential rain pummelling the roof of the house. For a second she thought there was a leak in the roof, feeling moisture on her face, but quickly realised she'd been drooling in her sleep.

"Gross," she said, peering around groggily, her eyes hurting in the sudden glare because she'd left the lights on in the bedroom. She reached for her glasses, which she'd unconsciously folded neatly on the nightstand, and just as unconsciously now located and put on through habit.

Scattered about on the bed and tumbled onto the floor were the ruffled and bent remains of the magazines she'd used as stimulation to masturbate. The folded and crinkled faces of the women were less attractive now, their gazes filled with mutilated accusation. Breanne ignored them, not wanting to deal with anything that heavy without some coffee.

A breeze blew through from the adjoining en suite bathroom, sending a shiver through her whole body as it caressed her bare legs. At some point she'd kicked off her jeans, but she still wore a hoodie. She got up and pulled the jeans back on. A tingle of something resembling fear ran up through her feet as they touched the cold wooden floorboards, but she shrugged it off, aware she was often on edge when first waking up. It was all too easy for her dreams to blend with reality, creating a vulnerable borderline between wakefulness and sleep where the two were indistinguishable. It was a fragile state which was not at all helped by the bucketing rain that pelted the house, drowning out all other noise.

A quick inspection through the curtains revealed little except it was indeed raining and that night had fallen.

"How long was I asleep for?" she asked no one, heading to the kitchen to make coffee. She didn't glance at the clock on the microwave. Its glowing numbers would only accuse her of bad sleep patterns and of drinking coffee at inappropriate times.

As the coffee machine did its thing, she looked at the windows of the kitchen. This wasn't normal rain. It was as if the glass was being assaulted with water, flung at it like a weapon. Something heavier smacked at the window with a flash of silver. For a second Breanne thought it was lightning, but when the phenomena repeated, she got a glimpse of something utterly strange.

It was a fish, slapped against the glass as if she was witnessing some surreal exhibit at the Museum of Old and New Art in Tasmania.

"No," she said, frowning in confusion, "not even this is as weird as that house made of hair or the fake flowers constructed out of duck tongues." An involuntary shiver ran through her as she remembered those surreal art pieces. "Fuck, that place was fucked up."

Not to mention the machine that produces human shit.

Memories of those exhibits made her feel better, and worse, about her own art, knowing she could produce something more meaningful and inspiring—not to mention less disgusting—but that even if she did, she wouldn't be on display in one of the biggest galleries in Australia.

"And yet that wall of plaster cast vaginas is."

Oh, wait, I liked that.

The coffee finished pouring. She was lifting it to her mouth when a colossal roar sounded, which carried over the heavy pounding of the rain. It was as if some monstrous beast was striding across the landscape, voicing its disapproval of humanity, announcing its intentions to crush the civilisation which had displeased it.

That reminds me, thought Breanne, suddenly remembering the dream she was having before she woke up.

There had been a monster in it, a giant lizard. No, wait, was it? I seem to recall it shifting, reconfiguring like the pieces of coloured glass seen through a turning kaleidoscope.

Like all dreams, it twisted and changed both in the experience and then again in the remembering of it, the contents made of the same shapes, yet arranged differently each moment, the colours realigned.

It became some type of cocoon, then a butterfly or something similar... a humongous moth perhaps?

The monster looked fuzzy around the edges, and the patterns on its wings stretched and morphed until they became the tentacles of some other creature. These evaporated like tendrils of smoke, twisting and dissipating in the air. Then, like the memory of the dream, they were gone, lost in the hazy steam vapours rising from the mug of coffee in Breanne's cupped hands. But the roar was still there, carried on the air like the winds of a cyclone, the monster howling its cry of vengeance.

To escape it, Breanne hurriedly turned on the television. Its soft glow was soothing in the gloom of the living room. She sunk into the warm embrace of the sofa and let it hug away the fear. Coffee in one hand, sipped appreciatively, she flicked through the late night channels. Disappointment mounted as she realised there was little on except for infomercials, news updates, and old movies. She skipped past the news, which simply seemed to be confirming that the weather was indeed dreadful, and made her way through a series of unsatisfying snippets of dated films. There were black and white Westerns, and a nineteen seventies heist one, as well as some foreign films with subtitles. She picked up her pace, changing channels each second, hoping something would grab her eye.

When it did she nearly jumped out of her seat and had to be careful she didn't spill coffee all over herself. She changed the channel back a couple of clicks to find the one she sought. It was a Japanese movie featuring a monstrous lizard destroying a city. Breanne sat enthralled, with her coffee paused on the way to her lips, and watched as the reptilian monster stomped cars flat and smashed buildings to rubble. Power lines sparkled in bursts of electricity as they tumbled. Petrol tankers were flipped like toys, exploding in huge fireballs, through which the lizard emerged unscathed to wreak further destruction.

This carried on for a few minutes, and Breanne was starting to lose interest. Her finger loomed over the change channel button on the remote, when, to her utter astonishment, a huge moth creature flew onto the screen, swooping over the destroyed city. Its wings expanded wider than the lizard was tall, revealing colourful patterns that touched something deep in Breanne's subconscious. Mesmerised by the soft, benevolent beauty of this creature in contrast to the hideous and violent reptile, she watched with renewed interest as they circled one another, an epic showdown in the making.

Then a loud bang like an epic thunderclap rocked the house with such intensity Breanne hit the roof, springing from her seat in one motion, throwing the scalding coffee into her own face.

"Fuck!" she screamed, barely hearing herself over the noise, which seemed to take long seconds to come to an end.

"That hurts, ouch, fuck," she said, wiping her face as the hot liquid quickly cooled like sweat. She was breathing heavily, the sound of her breath loud in her ears. Forgetting the television, the sight and sounds of which seemed to blur into the background, she looked to the window and realised the rain had ceased. "What the hell was that?"

It wasn't a lightning strike. There had been no flash of light, and the sound seemed far away, yet far too loud for being so. Frowning, she looked around at the coffee all over her hoodie, all over the couch, already staining, and knew her dad was going to kill her. She slapped her thighs in exasperation.

"God, what now?" she asked the universe, sure this was the prelude to further disaster.

The electricity cut out and everything went black.

7

Heart beating fast, chest heaving, eyes darting around but seeing nothing—Breanne was having a panic attack. She collapsed on the couch, the cushions damp and reeking of spilt coffee. But such mundane sensations were beyond her awareness now, her skin on fire, sweat pouring out of her as she writhed about. Though it was pitch dark in the house, starbursts exploded before her eyes, projected there by misfiring neurons in her brain. She shuddered and fell off the couch. Not even the hard bang on the floor could penetrate through to her panicked mind, the sharp jab of pain on her knees and elbows lost in the miasma of mental agony.

Guts twisted, lungs burning, electricity scourging her skin and sparkling in her skull—she felt see-through, crystalline, everything fragile, her body sure to smash into a million pieces. With the rain ceased and the power out, there was little eternal stimuli to ground her in any reality other than the one conjured up by her thoughts, which had turned to horror, filling the darkness with dread phantoms which had no form or description.

It was a black fear, pure dread, not latched onto anything and yet attached to everything. Small sensations became large and told a nonsense story that she was in danger. Fight or flight mechanisms shot out sprays of adrenaline which could do nothing, take her nowhere, except to spasm helplessly on the floor, desperately reaching for something to cling to, some life raft in the sea of nothingness.

In time—and time expanded and contracted in her present state so that it had little subjective meaning—she became aware of voices. They soothed her in one sense, telling her that she was human. In her maddening panic

22

she'd forgotten herself, who she was, what she was. But in another sense, reminding her of where she was, and that she was having a panic attack, only deepened her misery. She began to moan.

It was an awful, soul-tearing sound, one of pure grief. A mother who had lost their child could have made no more of a gut-wrenching cry of loss. For Breanne, it was the mourning of her sanity, watching it recede in the distance, knowing there was a long night of terrible darkness ahead, with no one and nothing to soothe her, no distraction, and no voice of reason inside her head.

The voices were outside. But they were in other houses. Single words filtered in—candle, torch, lighter. They were interspersed with nonsense sentences which sounded like running water until she made out a single coherent string.

"Where's the batteries?" someone asked.

Soon after, Breanne saw a ray of sunshine. It wasn't the sun coming up, the night still dark. The beam of a torch in a neighbour's house shone out across the yard, reaching like a ghostly finger through the window panes, refracted by the many droplets of water left by the rain. Like a disco ball, the light split into a dizzying rainbow, spinning above Breanne's head as someone played the beam around.

Just as suddenly, the light went away, off to shine on someone else, to light their way, leaving Breanne in the darkness of her thoughts, all alone, still panting for breath, eyes unseeing, brain unknowing, a zombie trapped in a cycle of fear and false thoughts.

8

When the morning came, and the true light of the dawn sun peered through the gaps in the curtains like a curious onlooker, Breanne was feeling better. The panic attack had eventually spent itself, and after that, was replaced by the numbness of depression and exhaustion, followed by a fitful sleep, full of nightmares.

That damn lizard monster, she thought, trying to shake the memory of it, telling herself in the sobering light of day that it was make-believe, something found only in fiction. But the panic attack and the dreams had an awful way of making something so terrible and impossible seem viscerally real and present.

Breanne shuddered. Turning this involuntary action into a voluntary one, she shook out her limbs, trying to release some of the static electricity which had accumulated in her flesh overnight. Utterly sick of herself and her own nonsense, she resolved to make a hearty breakfast of scrambled eggs on toast, knowing from painful experience she needed to fortify herself and regain her strength after such a lengthy panic attack.

"That was a bad one," she said as she whipped up the eggs in a bowl with a fork, and got some bread out. "It's unfortunate the power went out. I could have used something to distract me from it."

The power's out.

She looked at the microwave, the screen devoid of its glowing green clock.

"That'd be right," she said, clanging the fork back into the bowl of egg muck.

Shoulders slumped in defeat, she dropped heavily onto a stool at the breakfast nook, glumly munching a piece of dry bread.

I don't deserve butter.

Even punishing herself with the lack of condiments didn't work. She immediately felt guilty for eating bread. The first piece was already gone, and she unconsciously reached for another. She looked at it in mute accusation and threw it on the floor in disgust. She and it had a staring contest, before she finally wavered, bent down and picked it up. She dusted it off a bit, thought about not eating it, then in an act of self-masochism, wolfed it down by cramming it into her mouth in a crumpled ball. She nearly choked on it, but persisted, and when it hit her stomach and blended with the piece already there, she tried to forget the whole business, because at least the bread settled the nausea from the panic attack.

"And now I can drink coffee without wanting to barf," she said, perking up a little at the thought of her drug of choice.

Until she remembered once more that the power was out, and then she really lost it.

9

A knock on the front door interrupted Breanne's tantrum. She'd been stalking the house like a stomping monster on a rampage, wrecking without breaking, not wanting to do any lasting damage yet needing to vent. Cushions were flipped, chairs shoved, clothes tossed. She went down the hall and nudged the perfect photos of her perfect parents off kilter. She was in the process of slamming every door in the house when she'd heard the knock, and it made her pause, fresh fear springing physically into her body, driving spikes into her skin and rattling her spine like a chain.

"Hello?" she said, or perhaps it had been the person on the other side of the front door who spoke. There was an answer like an echo, repeated multiple times by herself and the visitor, both voices rising at the end further each time in questioning confusion.

Breanne touched the brass knob of the front door. It seemed to electrocute her, static electricity giving her a needle jab. She pulled her hand back, but immediately felt a little better mentally and physically, as if the metal had grounded her jangling nerves, loosing off the excess electricity shooting through her body.

She took the knob again—its metal cool and calming this time, without shock—and turned it, opening the door. The smile on the face which met her reached all the way to the wrinkles around the eyes.

"Oh, hi, Elsa," said Breanne to the old lady who lived next door. "What's up?"

"Are you alright?" asked Elsa, stepping into the house without waiting for an answer or invitation.

"Hold up a minute, the place is a mess," said Breanne, trying and failing to hide all the chaos by spreading her arms and moving them about.

Elsa bobbed and weaved with her craning vulture neck to see beyond these feeble attempts at concealment. "What's all this?"

Breanne let her arms droop by her sides like cooked spaghetti, rolled her eyes. "You know, living the bachelorette lifestyle."

"I don't think your parents would be happy if they saw the place like this." Elsa peered curiously at the crooked photos on the wall, as if she couldn't puzzle out how such a thing had happened.

"Are you going to tell them?" asked Breanne, a fist gripping her heart hard.

Elsa turned to her, smiled kindly again. "No."

The fist released, as did the breath Breanne hadn't been aware she'd been holding. "Thanks. I'll clean up. I promise."

Elsa laughed through her nose in a series of sharp snorts. "I don't care. I just came to check everything was alright. I heard all the banging and thought you must be in some distress over the flood."

"The flood?"

"Crazy rain last night, no? You should see the valley. Water up the wazoo."

"I haven't been outside."

"Some sight, though nothing new for us here. You can set your watch by the valley flooding."

"Yes, I know. I did grow up here, remember?"

"Now off to the big city to study… what was it again?"

"Art."

"Well, that's useless."

"I'm aware," said Breanne in a deadpan, wondering what it was that Elsa was doing with her life, or had ever done, that was so important or useful.

Elsa continued her tour of inspection through the living room and kitchen. "Looks like you've torn the place apart, searching high and low for something to eat, eh?"

Breanne crossed her arms defensively, the comment making her feel fat. "Hardly."

"Smells like stale coffee in here." The old woman sniffed around, nose poked out, as if she were a hound on the trail of a scent. It led her to the couch, where she saw the stain. "What a shame, your dad will go bananas when he sees that."

"Don't remind me. That was my last cup too."

"Hmm, what's that?"

Breanne pointed at the coffee stain. "My last coffee, and now the power is out I can't make any more."

"Come round my place any time. I have a gas stove. We can boil some water and I'll brew you a cup."

"God, yes please, can we go now?" said Breanne, her eyes lighting up.

10

"You weren't bloody kidding about the floodwater, were you?" said Breanne, standing on Elsa's back veranda, which had a splendid view out across the valley, now a shimmering sea of water, its surface dancing with the light of dawn. The beauty of it belied the destruction it represented, the lives ruined, the property damaged.

"Watch your language," said Elsa through the kitchen window as she fussed with the gas stove.

"What, bloody? That's some damn old-timey swearing, if you want to count that one."

"That too!"

"Damn, you think damn is a swear word?"

"Of course."

There was the sound of a match striking and the whoosh of lit gas, followed by the clank of a kettle placed on the stove.

"I'll try not to drop any C-bombs then," Breanne muttered to herself.

"What's that?" asked Elsa, joining her on the veranda.

"I said do you have any Iced Vovos?"

"That's ironic, criticising me about old people swearing and then requesting granny biscuits."

"Well, do you have any?"

Elsa winked, eyes sparkling mischievously. "I'm a granny, aren't I?"

She went to fetch them from the cupboard as Breanne's guts sank, realising she'd have to eat them now. The kettle screamed, which soothed her no small amount.

The drug is coming.

She went inside to supervise the making of this important cup. Elsa plonked a packet of Iced Vovos on the counter, and beside it, to Breanne's utter horror, a large tin of International Roast coffee.

Shit, she's pulling out the instant, and it's not even motherfucking Moccona. God bloody damn it all to hell. Kill me now.

"How many teaspoons?" asked Elsa. She popped the edge of the metal lid with a spoon and poised it over the fine brown powder within. She looked expectantly at her guest.

Just smile and say something normal, like two, thought Breanne.

"May as well tip the whole kettle in the tin and I'll quaff the caffeine rich sludge," she said instead, her mouth running well ahead of her brain.

Elsa frowned and said, "Okay... I think that means three." She heaped the powder into a mug. "Sugar and milk?"

With a strained yet mortified smile Breanne managed, "Black no sugar is fine."

The water was poured. She watched as Elsa murdered her own cup with a deluge of milk and sugar, the smell of which turned Breanne's stomach.

Elsa must have noticed something, as she said, "The city has turned you into a coffee snob, eh?"

"Oh! No, I'm sorry. Thanks. I'm very grateful. I was going nuts without my coffee."

"Yes, I saw your house."

Breanne frowned, changing the subject. "We're going to be cut off for a while, I suppose."

"Depends if we get more rain," said Elsa as they went out onto the veranda, sat in cane chairs. "It all seems so peaceful now, a nice sunny day."

Breanne pointed off into the distance. All was water between the hills on which their village sat and the distant mountains, with only occasional clumps of trees and tall buildings poking their heads above the surface. "I'm sure the people down in the valley aren't having such a nice time."

"They chose to live there."

"That's callous."

"No, it's accurate. Why do you think I picked this house on the hill?"

"Because you could afford to. The village isn't cheap."

"It was when I bought *my* house."

Breanne couldn't help but be repulsed by Elsa's sense of entitlement. For her own part she felt guilty she was high and dry when others were so much worse off. "This seems like a pretty bad flood. I don't remember it all going under this bad before."

"Yeah, could be as bad as the fifties. Maybe the seventies even. That was the worst one."

"What do you think is going to happen?" asked Breanne, making it sound as if she was selflessly asking about the valley as a whole but really meaning their village. Elsa's answer showed she took it as the latter.

"We do what we always do, we wait it out. All the roads are blocked. Unless you've got a boat or something, there's no way out and nothing you can do. We sit here and enjoy our coffee."

Enjoy is a flexible concept when it comes to instant coffee, Breanne thought, sipping the dirty water in her cup. She made a face—it tasted of waxy crayons.

"Did you see any fish?" she asked Elsa, almost absently.

"Fish?"

"Yeah, like, I don't know, washed up in your yard?"

"No. We're pretty elevated here."

"Maybe they got thrown in by the storm that caused the rain?" ventured Breanne, hoping to find some explanation which soothed her a bit, anything so the fish she'd seen the night before weren't some type of bizarre hallucination.

"Possible, I suppose. Why, have you seen fish?"

"Yeah," she said, not wanting to talk about the night she'd had, and all the visions of monsters she'd seen in her mind, both while waking and in her dreams. The fish seemed like the heralds of these monsters, announcing their imminent arrival.

Breanne swallowed the scalding hot coffee in a long gulp, ignoring the pain, badly in need of the caffeine.

"You finished that fast," said Elsa, pushing the Iced Vovo biscuits along a small table between their chairs. "Have a biscuit."

"No thanks, I've got to get back."

"But I opened them for—"

"I've got plenty of food at home," said Breanne, getting up.

Not that I'm going to be eating any of it in a hurry, she thought, backing away.

"That's good. If you want another cuppa, come over anytime."

"Don't worry, I'll have the shakes in about three hours and need a fix."

"Maybe you should use the flood as an opportunity to quit, or at least cut back?"

Maybe you should shut the hell up, Breanne snapped harshly in her thoughts. Out loud she said, with a fake smile, "I think we all need our little comforts at a time like this."

Elsa nodded at the wisdom of this.

And my number one comfort is being alone, thought Breanne, taking more steps backwards off the veranda.

"Bye for now," said Elsa.

"Yes, I'll see you soon," said Breanne, hating that she meant it, her addiction to coffee forcing her into proximity with other humans. She resented having to rely on anyone.

11

"They have to be here somewhere," said Breanne, scanning her backyard, searching for any sign of fish. "I know I didn't imagine them."

Finally when she was about to give up, she found one propped up in a hedge. It was a large fish, with a slick silvery sheen to its black body. Though it had long since drowned in the air, its mouth and eyes were open in a way which resembled life.

With courage she didn't know she possessed, Breanne grasped the fish in both hands, lifted it from its unnatural perch. It felt both slimy and dry at once, and surprisingly heavy. She looked it in the eye. The gaze was glassy and fixed, seeming to bore into Breanne, as if she were responsible for its death. As she struggled with its weight, her arms shaking, the mouth of the thing moved, speaking an accusation which was inaudible at first, but rose in volume each moment.

A few seconds later, Breanne realised it wasn't an auditory hallucination she was hearing. She dropped the fish. It landed with a splat on the brick path winding through the hedges. Still it spoke, its voice getting louder and louder until it was a howling whisper in her ears like the passing wind. She tried to listen to what it was saying. It had no words, though its meaning was clear: something was coming. The fish was warning her.

The monster… it's real and it hungers, she thought, the pure terror of her imagination filling the gaps with words of her own.

A moment later, a massive concussive bang, similar to the one in the night yet even louder, slapped into her ears and knocked her from her feet. Rendered unconscious, she flopped down next to the fish.

12

In her unconscious state, Breanne's mind floated much closer to the primordial heart of the Earth. She saw a second sun there, rotating like a thinking cosmic mind, or beating like the functioning heart of a living beast. Lava flowed from it, either as blood along rocky veins, or as electrical messages along neurons, shooting out to the ocean beds, there to vibrate to the surface through the water, announcing the imminent arrival of a God.

These pulsing ripples were sensed by high tech scientific instruments in the possession of the world's militaries. Concerned by this puzzling data, they decided it must be kept secret. The alarm was not raised, the public not informed. Instead, they waited and watched in mounting horror as something impossible happened—the Earth gave birth. Deep in the ocean the second sun pushed its way through the crust, lava cooling across the skin of this burning core to form the body of a monstrous lizard Kaiju.

Making its way up to the ocean's surface, it shocked government agencies with its gargantuan size. Orbiting satellites snapped photographs which were immediately coded top secret, their veracity argued in emergency meetings the world over.

As the monster headed east through the Pacific Ocean, nothing could stand in the path of this bestial force of nature and remain unscathed. Where it trod, islands were crushed. Where it breathed, huge swathes of sea life were evaporated by a brilliant beam of fiery energy from its mouth. As it swam across the wide waters of the ocean, a massive tsunami was generated, pushed before it like the bow waves of a colossal ship. This first wave devastated coastlines and inundated islands, swallowing them whole. Pacific nations were swept into the ocean whole, their populations crushed and drowned, races of peoples disappearing in minutes.

No force of man or machine could halt the progress of the gargantuan reptile. Warships sent to confront it were smashed and sunk like the toys of a child throwing a tantrum in a bath. Intercepting fighter jets were swatted from the sky like swarms of annoying insects.

The chaos was spreading fast, and the only thing stopping the news of the monster reaching the wider world was the devastation its own passing had on the telecommunications network. World-scouring storms generated by the beast blocked the view of satellites and downed spy planes. Undersea fibre optic cables were severed by the clawed toes of the monster slicing them like cooked spaghetti. The internet failed, mobile phone networks collapsed. The weather stations which still functioned registered the phenomena generated by the monster as a category five cyclone, and this gelled well with the cover story of the military. The public remained blissfully unaware a monster stalked the Pacific. Any who did witness it did not live to tell the tale.

A huge fleet of ships, the combined strength of several of the world's most powerful navies, was mustered and thrown into the fray, only to be sunk en masse, the Kaiju belly-flopping on top of them. The massive displacement of water spread across the Pacific as if the ocean had been struck by a meteorite. The resulting tsunami ripped strips off continents, clawing millions of tonnes of soil into the sea, whole cities disappearing with it. The sound of it crashing against the Australian coastline was like a bomb going off. It echoed through Breanne's mind like a reverberating slap to the head.

She watched as the tsunami tore inland, further inundating the valley her village overlooked, already covered by the waters of the first wave. This second dread wave gouged a huge chunk out of the East Coast—some thirty kilometres distant from where she lay—and carried it back into the sea like a prize claimed by a victorious enemy. It was awful to see, her mind's eye zooming in on individual scenes of torment and agony as the lives of humans and animals were ended indiscriminately.

But what was worse than all this death and destruction, all this primordial chaos Breanne saw in her subconscious mind, was that she sensed the monster which caused it had an ego. Burning with ravenous desires and megalomaniacal goals, it wanted to eat, to feed on the power of yet another sun, the twin of the one at its own core. She could feel the ambition radiating off the monster like a feral heat, its need to ascend further in the pantheon of the Earth a palpable energy. This was more than a monster, it was a deity.

And it had a name: Godrisaur.

13

Breanne's eyes blinked open, groggily banishing the flashing stars of rainbow light which crowded at the peripheries of her sight. With them went the visions she'd seen while unconscious, where the past and present blended into one organic whole so that even the future seemed fused to it, inevitable. Her own death was the natural extrapolation of all she had witnessed.

"Godrisaur," she croaked, speaking the name of that death.

It's coming for me, coming for all of us, a pessimistic voice spoke in her mind, one she normally heard accusing her of being ugly. How foolish all that seemed now.

She got up, noticing the fish was gone. "Dragged away, a meal for a stray dog, I suppose."

What a fate, to be eaten by a hungry beast, nothing but a hunk of meat and blood. Is that what will become of me?

Turning to take in the view from her parents' backyard, Breanne was not surprised to see the valley had taken further damage. The water there was more turbulent and brown than before, ripping apart the countryside as it ebbed and flowed in chaotic patterns.

Maybe I'll drown like the people down in the valley— swept into the sea, my body a piece of trash, gathering with that island of plastic that's meant to be out there somewhere.

"It doesn't amount to much when you get to the sharp end of things, does it?" she said to herself.

"What's that?" said Elsa from behind her.

Breanne screamed and spun. The adrenaline spike which coursed through her body physically hurt. She felt her heartbeat pulsing painfully hard at the base of her skull.

"Sorry to startle you, dear. Do you want a cuppa?"

"I'd kill for one, thanks," said Breanne, clutching her chest to try and still her overactive heart.

"No need for that. I give it freely. Black no sugar, right?"

"Right."

14

"What have you been doing all day?" asked Elsa when they were settled back in the cane chairs with their coffees. Breanne noticed the Iced Vovos were conspicuously absent, which was both a blessed relief and, she suspected, some passive aggressive remark.

She shrugged and said, "Sleeping." It was kind of the truth.

Elsa pointed a gnarled old finger at Breanne's clothes. "Looks like you've been lying in a shrub."

"Fucking bloody hell," said Breanne, brushing grass and twigs from her hoodie.

Elsa clicked her tongue, but otherwise didn't remark upon the swearing. Breanne seethed but did her best to hide it, straightening her clothes. She felt itchy and was sure some of the grass was inside her jeans.

"What do you think that big bang was earlier?" she asked, trying to ignore the itchiness by changing the subject. She wanted to know if her experiences earlier were something shared by other people or were figments of her overactive imagination, triggered by the panic attack. It wouldn't be the first time such an experience had tinged every aspect of her reality with fear.

"That thunder?" said Elsa.

"Pretty loud for thunder," countered Breanne.

It knocked me clean out. Could a panic attack do that?

"And there hasn't been any more rain," she continued.

"How would you know?" asked Elsa.

"I would have felt it."

"Because you were sleeping outside in a hedge," Elsa pointed out unhelpfully. "Besides, the rain could've fallen further up the valley. It must have. The flood is getting worse."

They sat in thoughtful silence for a while. The sun was setting on the distant horizon, its red light tinting the flooded valley red so the water looked like a lake of crimson blood.

"What if it's not a flood?" asked Breanne.

"What is?"

"The water."

"Huh?"

"Never mind."

Elsa sipped her coffee. "I can only drink decaf this time of night."

Breanne went pale, looking at her own cup in horror.

"Don't worry," said Elsa. "You've got the real stuff."

"Good. I'd hate to die without one last proper coffee."

"What are you talking about? No one's dying."

"The people down in the valley," said Breanne, staring blankly into the distance.

"Wet feet is all."

"It's more than that, the water's higher."

"Okay, wet knees. They'll live."

Another silence, during which the light on the horizon became a single pink slither, then faded to darkness as the day ended. It was replaced, however, by a new, brighter source of illumination out at sea, yellow and brilliant.

"What's that light?" asked Breanne.

"I don't know," said Elsa, absently, waving it off. "Are you staying for dinner?"

The light swept across the flooded valley like the passing bright beam of a lighthouse. When it touched the dry land of some exposed hilly country covered in trees, blooms of red and orange fires erupted instantly.

"Whoa!" said Breanne, jumping to her feet and pointing at the hill. It was connected by a series of ridges to the one on which their village sat, and wasn't too far distant. "Did you see that?"

"See what?" Elsa got up to clear the used cups.

"That hill burst into flames. Look, those trees there."

Elsa turned, peering like a turtle into the night. "A bushfire? Well, I'll be. You'd think with all the water around that'd be impossible." She chuckled and opened the door to the kitchen door. "Australia, am I right?"

"That light caused it," said Breanne, but the brilliant beam was gone, having disappeared as quickly as it had appeared. The fires remained though, and they were spreading fast through the woods on that hill.

"Curried sausages alright?" asked Elsa through the window.

Ew, what? No, thought Breanne.

"Sure, Elsa, whatever's going," she said, but didn't offer to help. Instead she watched the fire creep along the ridge like a fiery caterpillar as Elsa clucked in disappointment in the kitchen, cutting potatoes by lamplight.

15

Back in her parents' house, Breanne sat with a torch she'd borrowed from Elsa, ostensibly to search the cupboards for a torch of her own and then return it. But her mind was elsewhere. She fidgeted in the dark, hands tapping and feet bouncing, her thoughts dancing between the monster, the beam of light, and the bushfire. Cycling from one to the other, she tried to figure out how they were connected, if at all. There wasn't really any evidence they were related to one another.

Or even evidence that the monster exists, beyond what? You saw it in a dream or something? That you're afraid? Think, damn you. Use logic. It's just the panic attack and the unusual situation. You've got the fear in your blood, you saw that monster movie, and now you're connecting that to what you're feeling.

"And that light could have been a mirage, some trick of the setting sun. Maybe it was a slither of the moon, who knows?"

But the fires had started when the beam had passed over the trees.

This thought was giving her a steady grounding, a reason to not dismiss it all. She knew she was remembering right.

Or am I?

"And what about that fish, as well as the roar? The roar was real, wasn't it? That wasn't just the wind or the blood rushing through my head."

Fish can't talk though.

"It was probably my own voice, speaking to me like I'm speaking to myself now. I'm creating this. I'm making it up."

But it's no less real for all that.

She knew there was only one way to prove it was real, and that was to get a better look at what was out there. But she didn't have a car, and even if she did, it's not like she could go driving around with all that water clogging up the valley.

Not to mention the corpses.

She pushed this thought away in disgust, like she was nudging one of these floating bodies away with a long pole, trying to stay well clear of such messy realities.

And yet I want to go out and hunt down some monster?

This made her dismiss the idea of walking along the ridge to check out the bushfires.

And what would be the point of that anyway? Watching a forest go up in flames? I could do that from here.

"Wait, I can do that from here!" she said, grabbing the torch and flicking it on. But she didn't go out to the backyard to watch the fires. She'd already done that, and it was a surreally beautiful, yet pointless exercise at this distance. Instead, Breanne went to her father's study.

Opening the door took some courage, flying in the face of everything she'd had drilled into her as a child: don't go into Dad's study by yourself, and, if invited in, don't touch anything. She was about to violate both these rules, and while the consequences seemed distant and a non-issue—she was a grown woman, damn it—the psychological conditioning was strong.

Despite being the only one home, she turned the doorknob slowly and carefully, agonising over the need for total silence and secrecy. The latch gave a tiny whine of protest, very quiet, yet loud to Breanne's ears. It was almost enough to deter her, but she paused, took a deep breath, and pushed on, inching the door open slowly.

There was another moment of resistance when the door was about a foot ajar where it felt like she was going to turn back. If she closed the door again now, then nothing bad had happened, there would be no accusations, no betrayal, and no consequences. But was this really true? She had the absurd thought that her father could lift her prints off the doorknob, thus proving her guilt with hard evidence. She had a quick and ready excuse for this. She'd been cleaning the door, and it'd been slightly ajar, so she closed it, and...

Can you get a fucking grip?

With this sobering thought ringing in her head like a rallying cry, she gave the door one last shove. It seemed to cross a magical threshold where everything was easy and suddenly she was in the forbidden room, flashlight scanning for the object which she knew was in here, having seen it on one of those precious yet terrifying invited visits.

Neatly arranged on polished wooden shelving and hung on the walls were all types of Navy memorabilia: framed maps, brass compasses and sextons, historical and contemporary photos of ships and crew, medals and rank badges, tied knots glued to boards. Smaller nautical-themed items—as well as a precious and fragile ship in a bottle—stood on the mahogany desk which dominated the room. Behind which was the only chair; this was where Breanne's father went to be alone.

The study was a strange room at the best of times, but with each of these items illuminated in turn—brought to life like a spectral ghost by the torch beam then retreating into gloom once more as she moved on—it took on a spooky feeling. The guilt Breanne felt in being there flooded back, carried in on a now-familiar wave of fear.

This feeling built to a nerve-racking crescendo as she reached the final item in the room, the one she had come for. As she played the torch over it, gliding along its elegant lines, the tension broke and her eyes lit up in triumph. Standing atop a wooden tripod nearly as tall as her was a vintage brass telescope.

She rushed to it. As she reached out to touch the brass tube, the static electricity which had been plaguing her recently sparked once more, repelling her, as if warning her to stay away.

You won't like what you see.

Shaking her head to clear this intrusive thought, she pushed on, forcing her way through the barrier like she had with the door, sure once she was over the threshold everything would give way and all would be clear. The fear would leave her, there would be no damning reprisals, and she could use the telescope, just this once. No one would be any the wiser.

But you'll know. Know far too much.

She grimaced, feeling more than ever that the voice in her head was not her own. Gritting her teeth, she extended her hand. It hovered over the brass tube of the telescope. All she had to do was let go, give in to the drag of gravity, and her hand would rest upon it. An even stronger force was repulsing her, willing her to stay away.

"Can you fuck off out of my head for once?" she said, aiming the words at her father. Her anger was enough to free her, but also damn her, as her fingers fell upon the icy metal casing of the telescope, sending a chilling tingle through her whole body.

For a second after this—long enough to convince her it had all been in her head—nothing more happened.

But then her eyes closed and her mind opened. She saw her parents, both their faces overlaid with a third. It was a terrible visage, a reptilian face of horrible, monstrous   proportions.

16

She pulled back as if the telescope was not cold anymore but burning hot. Her fingers quickly forgot the pain but her mind was not letting go of it so easily. It replayed the sensation of touching fire over and over, the phantom agony spreading until it stretched over the entirety of her skin. Ripping off her clothes, she ran into the bathroom and jumped in the shower, fumbling with the faucets until a freezing spray of water washed over her. Her mind flipped one eighty and a psychological term she had heard—enantiodromia—appeared there in bold lettering, one moment in black, the next in white, then flashing between the two so quickly it was as if each contained the essence of the other.

The cold water was doing something similar to her skin, the burning and freezing combining to make a balanced whole. For a blessed moment, she had peace. It was a fleeting moment of clarity, but it didn't need to be long to have an impact, shattering previously held beliefs into shards. But those shards, though broken, remained, and they lodged deeper into her with their jagged edges, the pain transformed.

Turning the water off took an act of almost impossible willpower. She was unaware of how much time had passed. Stepping from the shower, Breanne felt as if she was emerging from a cocoon, a silken, invisible skin sloughing off her body. The confronting visions she had seen were gone, replaced by an uneasy peace between two forces, one that could be broken by either side at any moment. With her bare feet touching the bathroom tiles she felt as if she were made of spun glass, the gossamer threads of her being so fragile they could shatter in the slightest breeze.

And what was coming was more than a slight breeze. It was a cyclone force, shredding her life into pieces as the Australian Navy—and her parents with it—struggled to mount any defence against Godrisaur.

The panicky tension built in her blood once more, and she knew there was only one course open to her, only one way to find out what she needed to know. Not bothering to put any clothes on, she went back to the study to fetch the telescope.

17

She wasn't expecting to learn about her parents through psychometry—the mere act of touching the telescope was not going to yield up information through psychic means. But the telescope could be used in a much more mundane fashion—she could inspect the coastline, see if the Navy was out there.

Picking it up, there was no jolt of electricity, no flash of visions, and she was frankly thankful for this. While she was desperate to learn of her parents' fate, it wouldn't do to let her mind fill in the gaps with her imagination. She wasn't going to let Godrisaur infect her thoughts further if she could help it.

She bundled the tripod legs together and collapsed the telescope tube, folding it flat against the legs. Tucking the whole thing under her arm, she carried it outside to the dark backyard, oblivious to the absurdity of her appearance—a naked young woman with a naval telescope—and to the fact there were no fences in the village to hide her bizarre doings, only the obscuration of night time. She didn't care, too absorbed in finding a good spot with a solid view of the whole valley—the floodwaters shining in the pale moonlight peeking through grey clouds—and beyond that to the coast.

The telescope, while antique and quite expensive, wasn't a complicated piece of technology. Spreading the tripod out, Breanne planted it on the brick path, shifting it slightly here and there until it stopped rocking. She removed the brass cap from the end of the telescope, which hung loose on its own chain.

"That's the entire assembly procedure I suppose," she said and levelled the telescope at the horizon. Bending a little to peer into the eyepiece she found nothing but the darkness of night. Panning the brass optical tube back and forth she found odd spots of light—the cities in the distance—but they were blurry. Frowning, she aimed it at the fires along the ridge in the middle distance. These were less out of focus, but she couldn't make anything out but the vague colours of the fire, with darker vertical lines for trees.

She pressed her eye socket harder against the eyepiece and something gave way. She gave a little squeak of fear, thinking she must have broken it. But a quick inspection, and a fiddle with the smaller tube within a tube connected to the eyepiece, reminded her of the need to focus the instrument. She sighted the fires again, working the focusing tube in and out smoothly until the blurriness resolved into clarity. The enlarged image of the fires was seemingly so close, the flames burning so intensely, that Breanne pulled away, startled.

"You stupid idiot," she said to herself, and went back to inspecting the fires. She couldn't see much there besides a conflagration which consumed the forest in a frenzy of furious flames. It was hypnotic and beautiful, and reminded her of times her family had gone camping when she was a kid.

Back when my parents still had hopes of moulding me into a miniature version of themselves, interested in the outdoors and the military, she thought sourly, pulling back from the lens in time to see a flash on the coastline. Immediately she aimed the telescope at this spot. She had to work the focus in tandem with the direction, experimenting until she caught sight of the flash again. It was almost too bright to look at, but she forced herself to persist, and saw that it was a fat beam, far too wide in diameter to be anything man-made. It flicked on and off, as if speaking in some type of signal language like Morse code.

Looking up from the eyepiece, Breanne could see these shafts of light were striking all along the coast. Where they did, huge explosive fires erupted. She traced each blast back to its source, triangulating their angles, and found they emanated from the same location. She went to work, directing the telescope to this point. It was blurry at first, but she focused the image, though this provided not much more detail. At first, she thought she was looking at an island, a dark round mound silhouetted against the deep blue glint of the night time ocean. But the shape was moving, and she revised her guess, thinking it could be a ship.

Perhaps that's Mum and Dad out there after all, on a Navy vessel, she thought, but quickly dismissed this idea, at least in reference to the shape she saw. Taking into account the scale of landmasses around it and the distance, if it was a ship, it was utterly humongous. This left only one option.

She pulled back from the telescope with a gasp of realisation.

It was Godrisaur.

18

Spellbound, Breanne spent hours watching the monster. She'd thought it was huge before, but that was when it was mostly submerged, only its head showing above the waves. As it stepped up onto the continental shelf, additional bulk was revealed, a towering silhouette more akin to a mountain than any beast. The searing blasts of light shooting from its gaping jaws made it hard to look at. It was a flickering strobe light shape born out of an epileptic nightmare which got larger with each second, closing in on the coast.

When she thought it couldn't possibly get any taller, it strode ashore and onto dry land and stretched to its full height with a roar which shook the earth and made the clouds tremble. The beast rose heavenwards so impossibly far she was unable to look at the head with the telescope, the instrument not able to incline so steeply. Not that she needed the thing anymore. Godrisaur was clearly visible, a behemoth which dwarfed the skyscrapers which had survived its crushing tsunami onslaught. It seemed to take offence at these sentinels of civilisation still standing against it, sweeping its meaty tail around and levelling several streets worth in a single swipe. The remaining lights of the city became burning bonfires amidst piles of ruins in mere moments as Godrisaur stomped forward and levelled the rest with strikes of its mighty legs.

These fires were echoed in the glowing flesh of the monster itself, which emanated a fierce red and orange light through its scaly flesh now it was fully exposed to the air. Upon closer inspection with the telescope, Breanne could see that down its back were a row of round-based rocky spikes which resembled volcanoes, lava burbling from their tips and dripping down Godrisaur's spine.

She tried to find more details, but playing her magnified sight across the body of the thing was an exercise in futility, everything lost in the monstrous scale.

Until she came to the eyes.

They were fathomless pits of a fiery hell, portals to a nightmare realm of torture and pain. They were primordial spectres of a dead age, where monsters were common and mankind had no hope to live in their shadows. It was impossible to look into such eyes and see anything other than inevitable death, along with the destruction of everything one held dear and sacred. Here was a force to level civilisations, with a will to see every last wall crumbled, every last life snuffed out.

Breanne pulled back from the telescope with a gasp of shock and horror. There was little comfort to be had in this momentary escape from that terrible visage though, as she saw she was still staring down the barrels of those eyes, sighted from far away like laser beams fixed on her location.

Godrisaur took a single, purposeful stride forward, then another, and another, the massive legs sweeping a long arc with each pace, gouging fresh destruction with its clawed toes. The sound of the pounding footfalls reverberated in the air like a distant storm. The monster flattened all features—man-made and natural—beneath its impossible weight. Fires sprung into being in its wake, leaving behind a slug's trail of sizzling lava to scourge the land.

All the while Godrisaur's glowing red gaze projected an aura of ancient malice which seemed to Breanne to be aimed at her village. The head was locked in one direction now, its attention focused.

She took a few halting steps of her own away from the telescope. They were the shuffling steps of a transfixed mouse, pitifully small, utterly helpless to escape as the predator loomed large with hypnotising eyes. With each step backwards, she felt as if she was shrinking, curling up into a foetal ball of terror. With each step forwards, Godrisaur loomed larger, a God walking the Earth, come to claim its bounty of reaped souls.

With mounting, mind-bending horror, Breanne realised the monster was coming this way.

19

"No, not here," she said to herself, feeling the panic mount once more. She flapped her hands wildly. "This is the village. Nothing bad happens here. Not even the floodwaters reach this far."

She paced the yard back and forth, the grass cold and damp beneath her feet, failing to ground her in reality. Instead, she ignored all sensation, retreating into fantasy. She set her jaw in defiance of fact, jutting her chin out arrogantly.

"We... *I'm* above all this," she said, weaving an illusion of detachment, as if she could will herself free of any involvement in the wider world. She pointed at the valley. "That's where bad things happen. Down there."

She glanced back at Godrisaur. It was so tall it seemed as if there was no height it could not reach. Not even the heavens were free of its wrath. It evaporated clouds with the radiant heat of its fiery flesh as it passed through them. The floodwaters turned to steam and rose up, and through the hazy heat, Breanne could almost convince herself that the monster was a mirage, something her brain had conjured into being to trick her.

"You know what you're like. You always have to worry about something. You just don't want to think of your unfinished art projects," she said, her voice shrill and hysterical. "Yes, yes, that's it. That's all this is. I mean, it's a good excuse, isn't it? Sorry, I couldn't complete the assignment, Professor, there was a monster, you see, and..."

A Kaiju ate my homework.

She laughed maniacally at the thought, continuing until her whole body shook with delusional frivolity. For a second, she found release from the terrible burden of sanity, her head swimming. Feeling giddy, and suddenly forgetting what she'd been laughing about, she leaned against a tree. Goosebumps pricked up all over her body as she panted hard.

"Why don't I have any clothes on?" she asked herself, looking down. "God, I must be crazy, I—"

She was interrupted by the sound of voices next door. They were in Elsa's front yard. She crept up to the hedge which divided the two properties. Trying to be coy, she didn't peer over the top, suddenly feeling naked and exposed. Instead, she parted the hedge with her hands, made a little spyhole to satisfy her burning curiosity.

She gawped, not believing what she was seeing. Elsa was talking to a man in a frightful state. His jacket and hair were singed, wisps of smoke rising from them. He resembled a lit cigarette and stank just as badly. The exposed skin of his face, neck, and hands were covered in burns and soot, his features so obscured in mottled red and black he looked like some dreadful revenant, a zombie raised from a fresh grave. The soles of his shoes were melted clean away, the footwear's tattered remains clinging around his ankles, little more than disintegrating rags. His feet were blackened lumps weeping bloody pus. It didn't take Breanne eavesdropping on their conversation to realise he'd been through the fires down along the ridge, suffering a dreadful ordeal, barely escaping with his life.

And the man was not alone. The other person with him, a woman, was in an even worse state. Clearly wounded, she was propped up in the tray of a steel wheelbarrow. She groaned, lolling in and out of consciousness. Despite the ash which covered her and blackened her features, Breanne felt her breath catch in her throat at the sight of her. The woman's beauty shone through her present state. Beyond the sooty surface was a vision of everything Breanne wished to possess, either for herself or in the form of another. Here was a reflection of the unnameable things she saw inside which had failed to manifest in her outward appearance. This woman, despite the marring effects of pain and fire, was the piece of art Breanne saw in her own soul, brought to life in stunning detail.

Breanne felt the uncontrollable pull of attraction, leaning forward into the hedge. Only the spiky branches jabbing into her naked flesh brought her to her senses, and she pulled back, repulsed by the desperation she felt, which was repugnant to her, violating her sense of freewill.

But still she couldn't take her eyes off the woman, mesmerised by the aura of life she radiated even in her most vulnerable state. Breanne hated that the woman was hurt, her leg wrapped in a bloody rag. It made the attraction much more powerful, the desire to help in some way almost overpowering. Breanne had a bizarre fantasy where she rushed from the bushes to rescue the woman from the man, who had been carting her about like a sack of potatoes. She developed an immediate dislike for him which mirrored in a dark way the bright infatuation she felt for the woman. He was physically repugnant to Breanne and, she assumed, to the woman, who never could have consented to being manhandled in the fashion she was, Elsa and the man lifting her from the wheelbarrow and loading her into the backseat of Elsa's car.

As Breanne prepared to act out her heroic daydream, bursting naked onto her neighbour's lawn to save the day, the ground shook as if from an earthquake, followed by a huge roar, louder than ever. She froze on the spot, her guts flipping in involuntary fear. The monster was making its way across the valley, coming their way.

But she had a reason to be brave now, someone to care about in a way she didn't care about herself.

Swallowing the lump in her throat, she pushed it all the way down into her sour stomach. There it festered, sure to cause problems later, but for now she could ignore it. The blinkers were on her vision. All she saw was the woman, sat propped up in the backseat of Elsa's car.

If I make a dash for it, I could…

Elsa and the man were distracted, discussing the noisy phenomena of the monster as they got in the car, the old woman still convinced it had some type of natural cause. She reversed the car down the driveway and drove off.

Hunched in the hedge, eyes wide and unblinking—lest she lose track of them—Breanne kept careful watch on the course of the headlights as they wound through the village. Further up the hill they ascended the steep driveway of a house with a green roof. It was surrounded by a pair of rock retaining walls which made it resemble some type of medieval keep.

It will be difficult to get in there, thought Breanne, not referring to the stone barriers as much as the simple social awkwardness of blustering up to the house, driven by nothing more than an entitled sense of lust and a series of absurd reasons which bubbled up into her mind. Sifting the most plausible of these excuses for her future intrusion from the most outlandish, she went back into the house to put on some clothes, preparing for a totally normal encounter with nothing weird about it at all.

20

Fuck, why do you have nothing to wear? she asked her former self, cursing her out for not being more fashion conscious. Defensively, she had a retort to spit back at herself while she tossed one rejected item over her shoulder after another. "I'm an art student. We don't have money for new clothes."

Yeah, but you're meant to be into rummaging around thrift shops for hidden gems. What type of alternative arty freak doesn't go op shopping?

"Have you seen the prices in op shops lately? They're getting bougie these days."

Now you're going to look like a slob when you meet her.

"Did you see the state *she* was in?"

Yes. She was beautiful. You wouldn't look any good even if you had access to all that crap your mum does.

She was about to tell her mind to go fuck itself when she realised.

"Hey, I do have access to all that crap. I'm in her bloody house!"

There was a moment's pause as she moved towards her mother's walk-in wardrobe. But Breanne had already violated the sanctity of her father's sacred space tonight, what was one more crime piled on top?

She heard a roar from outside and decided this was Godrisaur giving her its tacit approval. This set her off on a hysterical laughing fit, the ironic absurdity of the situation mixing with a mortal fear short-circuited by mania. Her mad cackling continued as she tore into the wardrobe like a whirlwind, dresses, shoes, and everything else she could ever need tossed around without a care as she sought the items which would make her irresistible.

21

"Well, you've tried on every single dress that comes even close to fitting you, with every combination of shoes and handbag. You've switched earrings and necklace combinations dozens of times…"

Breanne looked at herself in the full length dressing mirror, sucking in her gut and puffing out her chest, standing tall in a way which didn't come naturally to her.

"…and you still look like a lump."

She slumped forward, arms dangling like limp noodles, with the posture of a hunchback and a gut like the pouch of a kangaroo with a joey inside.

We're still going even if you look like crap, so you may as well make up your mind.

The ground shook again, the roaring louder.

And we don't have all that much time left.

Breanne stood up tall once more, decided she looked utterly ridiculous in the red cocktail dress and high heels, and marvelled at the thought that she'd planned on holding the matching clutch purse for any length of time. She tossed the thing across the room, landing with the pile of other items she'd discarded in disgust. She kicked the heels off into the mirror so hard it cracked. Slipping out of the dress, she looked at her fragmented reflection, seeing multiple versions of herself, none of them perfect, all of them in pieces, which, when put together, didn't quite fit together to make a full person. But they were her nonetheless, and so she had to make her peace with who she really was.

She went and put on her own jeans and a Doctor Who t-shirt, both with the ubiquitous splatters of paint. Her one concession to an orderly appearance was picking her cleanest, paint-free hoodie. She had little choice about the shoes, owning only the single pair of battered Converse.

Turning her back on the broken mirror, she went into the adjoining en suite bathroom, looked in the intact mirror there. In it she saw a more complete version of herself, one she could present to the world without at least appearing like a fraud.

Godrisaur roared again, which she decided was it cheering her on. She smiled, giving herself a stiff nod of approval.

"Okay, let's go meet the love of my life," she said, and with those words a primal fear overcame her which nearly floored her, one much more powerful than any monster could provoke. She shook uncontrollably, but still she forced herself to the front door.

There were other noises outside now, a hubbub of conversation and shouts of alarm.

"Oh, so the neighbourhood has decided to finally acknowledge there is a massive fucking Kaiju stomping this way," she said, opening the door, if for no other reason than to look at the idiots.

The villagers were gathered in the streets, families with kids, old people, and teenagers huddled with their friends. Some pointed up and into the distance, mouths open in shock or to yell some type of alarmed invective. Others waved and called for their tardy household members to join them outside to see the incredible sight.

Breanne didn't need to look back down the valley. She'd seen the monster close enough through the telescope, and she didn't want to shit herself with terror now, ruining her last remaining shreds of dignity and self-respect. It was best to ignore the thing and live what remained of life with the one person she'd ever felt anything real for.

Besides, there was another sight to be had, one in the village, which interested her far more. Gliding down the middle of the street on a bicycle was the man Breanne had seen with the woman earlier.

22

"He's abandoned her!" hissed Breanne, taking a step out the door, her furious indignation making her forget her fear of Godrisaur, of approaching the green-roofed house, and of herself.

She almost chased after the man, wanting to drag him from the bike and scream abuse at him, questioning how he could ever leave someone so beautiful behind, even for a second. And where was he going? Where and what could possibly be more important than her?

But after that first step, she paused. He was already gone, sped away on the bike along the sloping street, off down the hill which led into the valley and Godrisaur beyond.

"He's going to die," she said in a dawning realisation, not believing her luck. "With him out of the way she's all mine!"

Breanne nearly jumped in the air for joy, but restrained herself with an effort, self-conscious now she was in public, with the whole village turned out, all of them in various states of shocked fascination and growing terror. The sight which confronted them was serious and life-threatening. It wouldn't do to look too happy.

Not that she cared what they thought of her. A long-time social pariah and family black sheep, she'd long given up on anything like that. But it was for these self-same reasons that she didn't want to draw attention to herself, have anyone stop her and want to talk to her. Conversations were difficult at the best of times. In her present manic state she'd do something stupid, and she wouldn't be able to tolerate any inane crap from these rubber-necking normals. Even with something as exciting happening as a monster coming to kill them all they'd still find some way of boring her to tears and making her feel awkward and different.

She pulled her hood over her head and did her best to move discreetly through the gathering throngs of excited and mystified people. Someone said something to her. She tried to ignore them, keep her head down and continue on, but a second person spoke to her, asked her some question relating to the monster. Breanne realised she was conspicuous exactly because she was trying to be inconspicuous. In a crowd full of people in awe of such an enthralling event as a Kaiju attack, she was the only one who was acting as if nothing untoward was happening. She wasn't even *looking* at the monster.

So she turned.

Godrisaur was much closer now, its gargantuan nature fully revealed in both the speed in which it covered the intervening distance and its utter domination of the skyline. It strode down the length of the valley, sending rippling waves out before it through deep floodwaters which didn't even reach its stout ankles. A bloody slash of light on the horizon announced a new day, with the monster a silhouette carved out of the rising sun bigger than any of the mountains which hemmed in the valley on its distant side.

This mound of dark rock and glowing lava, set against a gore-red dawn, was a creature so large, so powerful, it seemed nothing could stand in its path, no force could turn it away from the village. And yet, something had drawn its attention to one side, its head and sight no longer locked on the village but down at an angle, towards the road leading off into the valley and further inland. Those terrible eyes—burning embers set in lumps of black coal—were shifting like the minute hand of a clock, agonisingly slowly. Yet inexorably they moved further from Breanne.

She let out a breath she didn't know she was holding, turned her back on the creature, and ran up the street.

23

Reaching the house with the green roof was the easy part, now came the impossible—actually walking up the front steps. These ran up through a gap in the pair of rock walls which girdled the hill around the house.

"You think this is hard, wait until you have to talk to her," said Breanne, and the sheer terror provoked by the thought of ruining that all-important social interaction nearly sent her packing back home. But, drawn by a vision in her mind—the memory of the woman's sweet face as she lay helpless in that wheelbarrow—drew Breanne on. She lifted a leg, her foot hovering over the first step.

Glancing up at the house at the top of the stairs, its façade—with a pair of windows and a huge, dark front door—looked like the visage of an intimidating monster. The roof tiles were green scales draped across its head and down its flanks, stretching out to either side along the wings of the house to form the arms of the beast.

The ground beneath Breanne shook as a real monster approached, and this threw her off balance so that her foot came down to steady herself, falling on the first step. Another quaking movement from down the valley seemed to shove her in the back, giving her impetus. Her other foot fell on the second step.

An ear-splitting roar sent a spike of adrenaline through Breanne, Godrisaur urging her forward, herding her like frightened livestock before a stalking predator or benign cattle dog, but either way being led to the slaughter eventually. It sent Breanne jolting up the stairs like a puppet, her steps spritely with the violent jerks of pulled strings.

She reached the top, and a surge of euphoria tinged with nervous fear overcame her when she realised she'd done it, and that now she had to follow through with the rest.

"Who are you?" asked a man's voice. It was loud, with an angry tinge to it, and Breanne nearly fainted with the shock, her social anxiety going into overload, not capable of dealing with aggressive people. She turned to see an old man wearing boxer shorts and nothing else. He had that defensive and belligerent hunched shoulder stance old people have when confronted with something new and possibly threatening because it was unknown.

"Who the *hell* are you?" the man repeated, taking a step towards her. That hunched stance, with the arms cocked at the sides, made him look like a duelling gunslinger in a Western, ready to draw his pistols.

All of Breanne's carefully practiced lines, including the most absurd and bizarre ones, flew from her mind like startled birds through an open window, or tumbled out of her mouth as a string of useless, unintelligible sounds. She turned, went to jog back down the stairs. But Godrisaur loomed over the village, casting a dark shadow over everything, blocking out the dawn. With a deafening roar it sent a tremor through her body, both in sheer terror, but also physically, the air itself vibrating with the power of the noise now the monster was so close.

"Whoever you are, get in the damn house!" said the man, marching over. He grabbed her, his bony fingers closing on her arm like the pincers of a crab.

"Ouch, get your hands off me," she said, trying to pull away, but he was dragging her towards a door, where an old woman waited, ushering them in with frantically waving arms. Breanne kicked and screamed, and he picked her up bodily, wiry strong, and carried her inside. She felt like a sack of potatoes, the same as the woman had seemed in the wheelbarrow.

Is this what it means to be a woman when there's danger around? Men bundling us up and carrying us away, she thought. It wasn't without a sense of irony that she found herself wishing to be taken to the wounded woman so she could put her arms around her, lift her up, and take her away from all this.

"What *is* that thing?" shrieked the old woman, pointing at the monster.

Breanne tried to speak but found she couldn't, her lungs being crushed by the embrace of the man. Indignation surged through her, and as the man plonked her inside the foyer of the house she immediately turned to flee, but was prevented from doing so by the door being slammed shut, bolts clicked into place with the finality of being sealed in a dungeon.

"It's Godrisaur," wheezed Breanne, able to speak again now the old man wasn't squeezing her around the ribs.

"What's a Godrisaur?" he asked.

"It's that thing out there. What am I, a fucking biologist?"

"I don't know what, or who, you are, but you seem to know what it's called, so you're more of an expert than I am."

"A big lava lizard. Some type of creature from the depths of the ocean."

"That's not real," said the man with conviction. He seemed surprisingly calm and sure of himself, as if being right was all that mattered to him, regardless of anything else which might be happening.

Breanne went to the window, shoved the curtains aside. "Have a bloody look, eh? It's right there before your eyes."

He did indeed go to look, as did the old woman. They stared in rapt fascination for a moment. Then both of them started to shake as the reality struck home, triggering a primal response in their brains and bodies.

"Oh, my God, Marc's out there!" said the old woman. She was crying. The old man's face bunched up in rage.

"What the hell does he think he's doing?"

"Probably going to get killed," Breanne said, not able to hide the relish in her voice. The old woman let out a plaintive wail. The old man turned on Breanne.

"What the fuck's wrong with you, saying a thing like that?" he said, grabbing her once again with those crab claw fingers. He gave her an angry shake, and Breanne reflexively socked him in the face with a rabbit punch.

"Bugger me dead," he said, staggering. He winced around an eye he was squeezing shut in pain. He raised a hand to his cheek, nursing it as he backed off. Breanne relaxed the tension in her body a touch, lowered her fist, but to her surprise, the old woman stepped forward, shoved her hard in the chest.

"Don't you touch my husband!" she shouted, the words like the barked command of an army officer. Breanne went tumbling over onto the cold, hard tiles, banging her elbow. She hissed in surprise and pain.

"What's going on?" said a new voice from another room. Breanne knew immediately who it was. The touch of fear in the voice stirred her heart to fresh action.

"Don't worry, I'm coming!" she yelled, and both the old people looked at her like she'd gone mad. Their confusion turned to shock as Breanne leaped up, ran out of the foyer, and frantically searched the house. They followed after her, not able to keep up with her rabbit's pace, but attempting to.

"There's some crazy bitch in the house, Jain!" the old man called out.

Jain, thought Breanne, her heart swooning in her chest to learn the name of the woman she sought so desperately.

"Jain?" she called, dodging the old man as he tried to pen her into a hallway. "Jain!"

"Who is it?" asked Jain. Her voice was coming through a screen door out the side of the house.

Breanne didn't bother opening the door. In her frenzied haste she barrelled into the screen mesh. To her surprise, she bounced off what she expected to be soft and pliant mesh, something only flimsily held in place with a rubber seal around the edges. Tumbling to the floor with a series of curses, she rolled over onto her back. The husband and wife stood over her. The man had a wooden spoon in his fist.

He used it to point at the screen door. "Metal security mesh, dumbass."

"What are you going to do with that, give me a hiding?" asked Breanne, nodding at the spoon as she rubbed her banged elbows and knees, trying to clear the stinging pain.

"Not if you behave yourself."

Breanne's lips curled up in disgust to have a man say this to her, so she replied with venom, "And if I don't, what then?"

"Then I'll teach you some manners," said the old woman. There was a warrior's gleam in her eyes, mirrored in the flash of a large kitchen knife she held up for Breanne to see.

"Okay, I'll be good," said Breanne, swallowing hard.

24

"Now," said the old woman, "who are you and what are you doing here?"

"I'm Breanne."

"Hardly enlightening," said the man, going to the curtains and peering out at the monster. "It seems to be turning away from the village, going further down the valley, thank God."

The old woman rushed over to his side, looking over his shoulder. "But Marc's out there. I hope he's not in the path of that thing."

"We could go out looking for him," suggested the old man, but the woman shook her head.

"Don't forget we've got to look after Jain, which reminds me." She went to the kitchen bench, fussing with a gas camping stove. She lit it, filled a pot with water, which she placed on the smelly flames.

"Are you making coffee?" asked Breanne, perking up, eyebrows raised, hopeful.

"What? No, I'm boiling water to clean Jain's wounds."

"Oh."

"*Then* I'll make coffee. I need a cup."

"Me too."

"Just make yourself at home," sneered the old man sarcastically. "Okay, so you're Breanne. I'm Jacub, and this is my wife Amelia. Outside through the screen is Jain, my son Marc's partner. Marc, as you might have gathered, has run off for some unknowable reason."

"You should go after him, the both of you, like you said," suggested Breanne, adding, "After you make the coffee, of course. I can look after Jain."

Then I'll have her all to myself, she thought.

Amelia looked at her, searching her face with wise eyes, considering this, and said, "No, Jain needs us. And we don't know where Marc has gone. We go out there we're liable to get killed as well."

"Don't say things like that," said Jacub, putting a comforting hand on his wife's shoulder. "Marc isn't going to get himself killed. He's a smart lad."

"You saw that damn monster out there!" snapped Amelia.

"Yes, but it's heading away from the village now."

"And wherever it's going, Marc is going too, I can feel it."

"You couldn't possibly—"

"A mother knows." She shook off Jacub's hand, grabbing some packets of tablets, which she tore at fretfully, trying to open them. Jacub calmly took them out of her hand, slid the foil sleeves out of their cardboard boxes. "You want me to give Jain, what, two of these red ones, and one of these green and whites?"

"No, the other way around," said Amelia, pointing. "Those are the antibiotics and these are the painkillers."

"Okay." He took the tablets and a glass of water to the door. He gave Breanne a snarky look as he purposefully undid the catch on the security screen and opened the door. Breanne pouted in annoyance, the skin of her face going bright red.

"Thanks, Dad," Jain said weakly, taking the tablets and swallowing them with the offered water. The sound of her voice made Breanne's heart sing, and she got up, went outside to sit in the chair opposite Jain. Jacub gave her a look as if he didn't trust her to be left alone, but a call from Amelia inside sent him back through the door.

"What are you looking at?" Jain asked.

Breanne jumped in her seat in surprise, as if jolted by electricity. She'd been staring at the woman in rapt adoration, and was shocked to be caught in this unconscious act of devotion. She felt vulnerable and foolish, so she coughed, went to speak, her voice breaking high with nervousness as she said, "Nothing." She coughed again, fighting to lower the pitch of her voice. "Just you, I guess. Are you alright?"

"I've been better. My leg…"

"Let me look at it," said Breanne, putting her hands on the armrests of the chair to get up. Jain waved her down.

"No. No, thank you. Amelia and Jacub will look after me." Jain smiled, but there was a tinge of suspicion which crept from the edges of her lips up into worried crease lines around her eyes. "You still haven't told us what you're doing here."

"Elsa is my neighbour. She told me you were hurt," Breanne lied, and then thought better of it, as she realised Jain was watching her closely.

She's beautiful, but she's also smart, thought Breanne.

"I mean, I saw you and…"

I can't say his name. I don't want him to exist.

"Marc," offered Jain.

"Yes… him. I saw you were hurt and I wanted to help."

True enough.

"She said the monster is called Godrisaur," said Amelia, returning with coffee. Breanne took hers gratefully, and despite the fact it was boiling hot, gulped it down in a couple of swallows, desperate for caffeine.

"Godrisaur?" said Jain, going even paler than she already was, strained by blood loss and pain.

"Can I have another cup of coffee?" asked Breanne, ignoring Jain's question.

"No, you can't," growled Jacub. "And you'll be on your way soon."

"Do you want something to eat?" Amelia asked Breanne.

"She's not staying, and she sure as hell isn't eating my food."

"What if she does a few chores first?" teased Jain. She had a wan look on her face, already weak, but fading further as the painkillers kicked in.

"It's my food, too," protested Amelia.

"I'll not hear any more of this," said Jacub. "She punched me in the face. Remember that?"

"She's calmed down now," said Amelia.

"Because you threatened to stab her with a knife."

Amelia chuckled. "Well, she pissed me off. But I've calmed down too. Plus, she knows something about the situation, so I want to hear her out."

"I wouldn't piss her off again," Jain said quietly to Breanne.

"Me, you can piss off all you like, apparently, I've got no say. Man of the house and I got no say," said Jacub.

"Godrisaur…" Jain trailed off, her head nodding.

As if on cue, a huge roar shook the roof over the veranda.

"Maybe we should get inside," said Jacub, real fear returning to his face.

"It'll flatten the whole house if it wants to," said Amelia. She seemed eerily calm now, resigned to fate.

Or focused on helping her son even if it means her own life, thought Breanne, and she decided to spill what she knew, everything she'd gained from dreams or visions, or from looking through the telescope.

Amelia and Jacub watched her with laser focus, as if she were taking a lie detector test. Jain nodded occasionally, whether in agreement or drowsiness it was impossible to tell. When Breanne was done, Jacub slapped his knee.

"That's it," he said. "I'm going after Marc. Sounds like we're all fucked anyway, so we may as well die as a family. Damn him for running off."

"We're not fucked, thank you very much," said Amelia. "And I don't want you out there alone, I'm going with you."

"Then who will look after Jain?"

"I will," Breanne said, sounding overeager but unable to hide her enthusiasm.

"I don't trust this bitch worth a damn," said Jacub with a jerk of his thumb.

Breanne crossed her arms. "Charming…"

"No, he's right, dear. You're nuts," said Amelia in a soft, soothing voice, as if speaking to an ill person. "To hear you speak of that monster is to listen to the ravings of a madwoman. How could you possibly know all that?"

"I don't know. I see it in my mind."

"Just like Marc," said Jain. There were two tears streaming down her cheeks, one from each eye.

"Marc isn't insane," said Amelia.

"He's something."

"She's right about that," said Jacub.

"Jacub!" said Amelia, slapping her husband's shoulder.

"What? He's a weird kid. I still love him."

"*You're* weird."

"I must be, thinking of going out there."

The fear was ingrained into his lined face like dirt, but it was clear to Breanne that he cared about his son and was willing to move mountains to save him. Breanne knew, though, that there was no saving Marc. When she closed her eyes, she saw Godrisaur staring at her… no, not at her, but through her, at something beyond. She was a means to an end, an obstacle, or a step to be taken. The monster would use her up, just as it was using Marc. The real goal was behind them both.

A ray of sunshine cut across the house, illuminating the veranda.

"You can't help him," said Breanne, getting up. She walked around the front of the house, where there was a view across the valley, while Amelia and Jacub bickered amongst themselves. She looked briefly at the monster, a smouldering volcano given life. It had paused further down the valley, a decent distance from the village, and was hunched over something. She knew what it was, who it was, and it gave her no satisfaction.

He did it, she thought grimly. *He led it away.*

She closed her eyes again. Saw a bright darkness, with a light hiding somewhere beyond this veil. She was staring down the gullet of the monster.

This was what Marc saw.

It was what he saw as Godrisaur swallowed him whole.

25

Jain's cry of emotional anguish nearly broke Breanne's heart. It was the sound of a lover torn from the one they cared about by the most permanent and final of acts—death. It fell like a dark curtain over Breanne's heart in psychic sympathy, yet still she couldn't help but wonder.

How did Jain know?

It made Breanne marvel at the bonds of love, rousing in her a longing to be that close to someone, their souls tied together. And though she knew she had to be rid of Marc for Jain to ever love her, it still caused her grief to witness this tearing apart of the lovers' union.

I'll stitch you back together, Jain, Breanne thought.

With herself attached in the progress, of course—though she didn't dare even think this, lest Jain sense her less than noble intentions. Breanne shouldn't have worried. Jain was lost in blind grief, wailing inconsolably. Amelia and Jacub tried to calm her, back around the side of the house, but the crying went on. Breanne's face contorted in contempt, her shallow well of sympathy already dried up.

Get over him already. I'm here, aren't I? And I love you.

She looked at the rising sun. It blinded her for a moment. She shielded her eyes as they adjusted to the light of day, and when she removed her hand, she saw speckles in her sight. At first she thought they were floaters, dark spots which drifted across the surface of her eyeballs. But they grew in size over time, and they didn't disappear, no matter how much she attempted to blink them away. Their passage across the dazzling sun left a series of afterimages, an arc across the sky.

It was the flight path of planes.

They were sleek, angular craft, inky black, each shaped like a V. The formation of them—for there were many—was also a V, and this V was the wings of an even greater one. It was like a fractal pattern, stamping the clear bright day with their perfect shadows.

Curiosity made Breanne stay and watch, even though alarm bells triggered in her subconscious. Even Godrisaur tilting its head back and venting a colossal cry of triumph from its bellows lungs couldn't distract her. The planes were converging on the monster anyway, and she knew she was witnessing a historic moment, a final confrontation, if such a finale were possible.

She sensed deep in her soul the ageless, deathless nature of the monster, and she wondered what these planes hoped to achieve where all the others had failed.

As they swooped for their attack run on Godrisaur, her eyes were drawn to a single plane. It was no different than all the others, yet she sensed her bond with the pilot, felt the love there.

You're up there, aren't you?

Her father didn't reply, except to release his payload of nuclear bombs.

26

Breanne stood transfixed, her eyes locked on the monster as the tiny black planes swooped around it, birds of prey circling a high mountain. They disgorged a litter of dark dots which looked like rocks released from their claws, a noble attempt to kill a creature far larger through ingenuity and courage.

The bombs scraped the fabric of the sky like dirty fingernails, malignant black sunspots silhouetted against the dawn.

There was a pregnant pause where all sound seemed to be sucked out of the air. Into this empty stretch of pure silence came the first flash as the nuclear bombs struck home.

Impossibly bright, it stole Breanne's sight away like a thief whose black cape draped across her eyes.

Darkness.

27

Sound.

Breanne's scream was drowned out by a bang which punched her eardrums like fists. First there was awful pain, like someone had rammed spikes into both ear canals, and then came a sensation like they were being filled with gel which muted everything. Into this quietness came a high-pitched ringing.

More explosive bangs shook her physically, rocking her on her feet such was their sonic force, yet they were audible only as tiny echoes of the first, as if far away.

Long seconds later, a wave of air and debris swept over her, tossing her across the yard and knocking her down. It continued like the exhaling breath of a God, blowing her across the rough driveway, grinding her skin painfully. She felt like an abused doll being dragged around by an uncaring toddler and thrown in the corner when done with. Striking a tree, she was held upright against it. Even its wide trunk was bending under the forces sweeping through, but it held, and she was crucified upon it as wood chips and stones scoured her exposed flesh.

And the process repeated, wave after wave of explosions, the bangs like tiny pops in her tortured ears, but the shockwaves hitting hard, and she went nine, ten, eleven or more rounds with this pugilistic power of the Gods.

She clawed at her eyes, to at least see what was happening, but there was nothing but a bright sparkling darkness as the rods and cones of her eyes misfired, having been burnt out by the world-ending flash of brightness of the first bomb. There was no pain in her eyes at least, but the psychological pain was a torment.

Panic attack built upon panic attack. Her blood screamed with electricity, her mind raced in circles, unable to catch a thought other than the agony of her torn up limbs and torso as she attempted to shield her face. Her lungs struggled to get a breath in the fiery winds of hell which engulfed her, and when they did, it felt like she breathed in more dirt than air.

Then, as suddenly as it began, it stopped, and this cessation was so abrupt it was like another bomb going off. There was silence, of a type, penetrated only by that high-pitched ringing which felt more like a frequency of physical pain than a sound.

And, of course, there was nothing to see.

Nothing to see ever again.

28

Breanne fell forward on her face, her skin torn to shreds and burnt by radiation. She mewled around weakly on the ground, the pain growing each moment, and she wasn't sure if she was on grass, dirt, or concrete, proper sensation drowned out in the agony. She felt spikes covering her body. Whether these were from false sensory impulses, or from splinters of wood burrowed into her flesh, Breanne didn't know. The pain spread out across her exposed skin slowly yet inexorably like an expanding pool of blood. Her clothes hung off her in rags. The burning feeling intensified, a dial of torture being turned to its highest setting. She felt as if she had been lowered into boiling water.

Unable to stand the brutality of the sensation she was being exposed to, she opened her mouth to scream, but nothing came out. Nothing she could hear anyway. Her throat, hoarse from breathing in harsh dust and grit, was on fire. Her lungs were being carved apart by knives.

She screamed until her hearing returned, her agony forcing its way even through the damage her ears had sustained. It was like coming up from underwater, a fragile, fractured reality breaking over her, and though she was still blind, she grasped the air desperately, as if trying to cling to her sense of hearing like a life raft. It was a small island of solace in the darkness. The high-pitched ringing was still there, but it was fading into the background, replaced by a piercing shriek.

It was her own voice.

Venting her shock at this cruel twist of fate, it was a strained sound, thin like a stiletto blade, ramming its way through her ears and into her brain. There it jabbed the soft tissue folds of her consciousness, wheedling its way in between thoughts to block them communicating with one another. The neurons, already tortured by the pain sensations, sang a chorus of misery, making chords of anguish, the disaster of the situation spelled out in horrifying rhyme. It was an opera, a dirge of the dead and dying. The singing was not a sound; it was the speechless voice of mortality.

The end felt close. But it did not come, only more suffering.

29

"She's badly burned," said Jacub, the resignation and finality in his voice plain.

"Don't say that," said Amelia.

Breanne could feel the woman's fingers touching her skin gently, probing. The man's blunt jabs with his own fingers accompanied them, as if the two were playing an agonising duet upon an instrument strung with the sinews of her exposed muscles. They were a counterpoint, soft and hard, alternating and giving contrast. Yet both were as bad as the other, as they touched things which should not be touched, parts of Breanne which were exposed far too early in her young life, laid bare by the brutal force of the nuclear blasts.

"Stop," she managed, and she thought she said it quietly, pleadingly.

"No need to shout," said Jacub. "We're right here."

"Yes," said Amelia, "we're right here." She took Breanne's hand, squeezed it gently, crushing it in a vice of searing hot metal.

"We can't help her," said Jacub. "Fuck, will you look at that?"

There was still dust and debris falling. It peppered across Breanne's skin like stinging strikes of hail.

"The mushroom cloud?" asked Amelia, her voice still turned towards Breanne, rather than looking back at the awful majesty of the rising fireball consuming the sky. Though Breanne couldn't see it, she could imagine its angry colours, its rainbow toxicity, swirling and bubbling like a furiously boiling cauldron of radioactive ooze.

"There were so many explosions," said Jacub. "Do you think they took it out?"

"What?" said Amelia.

"Godrisaur," whispered Breanne, provoking a stab of hate in her heart. It poisoned the well of her hope even as a spring burst forth from deep underground, sourced from her soul. The trickle of water this hope represented was little more than four drops of bright, glistening fluid, but as each was spent, like a martyr's blood spilt on the battlefield, they spelt a name, letter by letter.

Jain.

"She's okay," said Amelia, and Breanne realised she must have said it out loud.

"Unlike that fucking monster, look!" said Jacub in triumph. It was a callous phrase to Breanne, mocking her blindness. She could hear the smile in his speech. She desperately wished to wipe it off his face.

"It's falling apart!" he continued. "Great chunks of the thing are tumbling into the floodwaters."

This gave Breanne no solace. She was falling apart herself. Already bits of her skin were sloughing away under Amelia's tender yet ignorant touch. And what was worse, she felt like the most important parts of her, her identity, her being, were going with it, as if they were only ever skin deep and were being torn away, to reveal…

Nothing.

Breanne was dead inside, a husk, hollowed out by pain. She drifted into unconsciousness, a blessed relief, a sanctuary from a reality which had become too harsh to bear.

30

Other experiences awaited her in the darkness, represented in vivid colours her true eyes would never see again. These weren't dreams or visions. They were life witnessed by another part of herself—something much larger than human—of which her conscious ego was only a tiny fragment.

The drifting shapes she saw there, hazy and indistinct at first, coalesced together, forming a tightly knotted ball of potential. With a silent explosion of expansive power, it was released. It was not a bomb, not an act of destruction. It was a creative act, a birth. It was the finger of a God pushing through from beyond the veil of the tenth dimension, pointing to a place in space-time it wished to influence and bestow its blessing upon.

This piercing of reality caused a ripple which expanded, eventually finding spherical form in the realm of three-dimensional objects. This form was a mere slither of its true being, just as Breanne was a slither of this thing she saw. Like a series of Russian dolls, the truth was hidden one within the other, so it would never be clear if what was seen was ever the actual end, the final reality, free of further subjective interpretation, or if it was just another layer, with yet another hidden beyond.

This spherical object—that was at least how her human perspective could interpret it—was something she was familiar with, something she'd seen every day and thought of every night. She'd witnessed its reflection in the bright face of the moon and saw its gossamer touch sparkling on oceans. It warmed her, fed her, and made the plants grow. It was a life-giver, a creator.

It was the sun.

And it was alive.

It hovered over the planet Earth, which was likewise born of elements drawn from other dimensions, splashing their colours across lower realms in an attempt to build something unique, a place to play and grow, experience from the ground up what it truly meant to be a God.

The pair—sun and Earth—were brothers, born of the same father. They were identical if seen from certain angles, yet had manifested as distinct forms, each with a separate sense of being. In spite of this they were tied together with invisible bonds, like two magnetic balls, dancing in thrall to each other, though one was the weightier of the two, just as the other was the brighter. One was expansive, the other laser focused, and it was never clear which was which.

The burning star was not far away from the heavy Earth, nor was it impossibly large. Instead, it was smaller and closer than thought of by the inhabitants of the planet. In fact, it was the diminutive twin. The Earth, with all its heavy, metallic power had taken hold of its light, etheric brother, grabbing it and looping it around its belly like a giant would take up a large snake and, wearing it like a belt, made it bite its own tail.

Thus eternity was ensured for both, even though they fought. All was in equilibrium, a cycle. And it was only in moments when the snake decided to open its mouth, roaring in defiance and biting with its fangs that something had to be done to restore order.

Both bodies had a consciousness, though they had no thoughts as humans had thoughts. Instead, their minds were a frequency, a pulse. It was a vibration which made patterns, projecting a will upon those in its sphere of influence.

This meant each other, as well as humanity.

It meant Breanne herself was nothing but their puppet, her strings pulled in a cosmic game too large for her mind to fathom.

31

Breanne was jerked awake by a sharp tug of movement. She opened her eyes but was met by darkness. More movement, hands on her limbs, lifting her, and the pain returned in full, a body glove of agony enveloping her like a second skin. The pain was immediately slapped away by the intensity of sound rushing in through her ears, filling her skull like a sloshing fluid. It was such a cacophony of unbearable noise, such a riot of different sounds that they drowned out the ringing in her ears. Whistling shrieks cut the air, followed by banging impacts. Breanne could only assume the end would soon come.

Amelia and Jacub were screaming and shouting, but their meaning was lost, and Breanne's only connection with them was their indelicate touch as they dragged her across the rough surface of the driveway. The pain returned like an itch on the brain, building and spreading once more until it was impossible to think straight. Breanne felt like she was on a torture device, and though the inquisitors of her own mind asked the questions, she could give them no answers, none that would satisfy them, and so they submitted her to new atrocities.

"Please," she begged, but the sound of her voice was drowned in another impact, much closer this time.

"Fuck!" shouted Jacub when the rumbling echoes subsided slightly. "That one hit the neighbour's place. They're dead for sure."

"Don't worry about them, get inside," said Amelia.

"Fat lot of good that will do us, a fucking giant rock squished their whole house flat."

What Amelia said next was lost in the shriek of more rocks flying overhead, and Breanne guessed from their sulphurous stench these weren't chunks of earth, but rather were hunks of rocky flesh from the destroyed body of the monster.

They might have blown it to bits, but those bits are having their vengeance upon humanity, she thought, feeling like she was floating above her body, looking down on it with eyes that weren't eyes.

Christ, but I'm in a bad way.

Pink burns covered her body, making her look like a raw newborn. The skin was further tortured and torn by a buckshot blast of splinters and tiny rocks, ripped from the earth and fired at her by the nuclear shockwaves. A trail of dark blood and ragged strips of blackened, sloughed off skin was being left behind on the driveway as Amelia and Jacub dragged her towards the cover of the house.

From her third person view, Breanne could understand why they were in such a desperate hurry. The broken pieces of Kaiju rained down like a meteor shower, pummelling the village to ruin. Some were large, so big they swallowed up whole houses where they landed. Others were the size of baseballs, thrown at impossible speeds to crush skulls and rupture bodies. Even tiny fragments flew like bullets, penetrating walls and scything down the villagers.

Those that survived the initial blast that is.

As Breanne's disembodied consciousness swept down towards the valley, she could see melted mounds of flesh which had once been people. Now they were amorphous pink lumps, or merely a smear of sooty ooze. They led like a trail of burnt offerings towards the epicentre of the blasts, where the biggest body of them all—that of Godrisaur—was a hollowed out wreck, little more than a concave husk, a cracked egg, with the shell crumbling down. Other pieces of it were still being sucked into the air by the updraft of the nuclear explosions, ready to rain down far and wide. The rest of it was scattered about like the ruins of a lost civilisation, the volcanic chunks of flesh cooling fast in the hissing steam of the valley's floodwaters.

The bombers were gone, flying—or fleeing—as fast as their supersonic engines could carry them, back towards the horizon and the seeming safety of the sun's light. What remained in their place was an ugly, expanding ball of swirling chaos, stretching across the sky like the canopy of a poisoned tree. This was the mushroom cloud, the harbinger of death. In its fiery heart was a roiling light, a flickering star, changing colour each moment. It spoke to Breanne without words, conveying a message of mutation and change.

There would be no more stability in the world, not now Godrisaur had come. And though it was dead— because what could be deader than this shattered corpse of broken rocks—the balance of the world was thrown off. A new star had been unleashed, one to rival the daytime sun. This was the essence of the monster, the heart of the Kaiju, its immortal core.

It rose up through the mushroom cloud, trailing a flickering stream of lights. These sparkled like fragments of glass caught in the sunshine. Breanne felt a pull, her own consciousness wanting to leave her body behind, go with them. For a moment, she gave in to it and let herself be dragged along by the current, leading towards this burning ball of brightness.

It would be so easy. I could find peace in that light, she thought, bedazzled by the second sun.

But its malignancy was apparent in its changing colours. Its light was false. It was not a saviour but a cancerous blight on the world. It was selfish and wanted to use her, so she pulled away, even though this meant returning to the world, to her body, to pain.

Her consciousness was sent tumbling down a vortex, sucked not into the light, but into darkness. She fell back into her earthly body with a thud of dead weight.

32

It was like being revivified by some mad scientist, a zombie brought back from the dead for unholy purposes. This wasn't life, only an echo of life, with half the senses removed, and the ones that remained turned up so high they pierced the brain like dreadfully painful spikes.

She felt the sharp tips of these spikes exploring her thoughts, jabbing at things which were best left untouched. She could hear crying, and it was a near certainty it was her. Lifting her hands to her face, she expected to find tears. Instead, the moisture there was blood, and the only weeping was the weeping pus running from her burns. Besides, she had no energy to cry, and there was little left to mourn, for her life as she knew it was already over.

And it had not been much to begin with.

"There, there," Amelia said. Breanne felt sure she was comforting her. But no, it was not her name Amelia spoke a moment later, but Jain's. And while this would normally have provoked some type of anger in her, jealous for the care and attention received by someone else while she was so grievously wounded, in this case it didn't, because to be reminded of Jain's presence was to be reminded of a reason to live. Breanne's love for Jain was the only thing which still remained of her from before. It was a beacon of hope, something to shine in the darkness of her blindness and carry her forwards. Towards what, though, she didn't know and couldn't guess. Life was an abyss now, empty and stretching off into the infinity of black she saw before her.

But I can face it if Jain is here. If only I could drag her into my world. But who would want to live here in the darkness and pain with me?

Pain… Breanne wished she hadn't reminded herself. It didn't come all at once, but built, piece by piece, reconquering each part of her body as she remembered they existed. It started with the outer extremities—the hands, the feet—and leeched its way in until it poisoned the core of her.

There it burned like a furnace—or a malignant sun—hoping to find something to quench its furious thirst, something to satiate its desire to escape the coils of mortal existence. Breanne wished desperately in that moment to die, to transcend to another plane. She wished to go with Godrisaur, and she feared she had missed her chance. She had made the wrong choice.

Now the tears came, falling down her face as she grieved for the freedom she could have had if she'd let go of life and joined with that rising star in the sky.

33

"It's fucking unnatural, is what it is," said Jacub, pacing nearby. His footfalls felt loud to Breanne as she lay on the floor, punctuating the ringing of her ears like a metronome. She wished he'd stop, and would have said something, but her throat was too dry, so she croaked like a stepped-on frog in protest against the thoughtless stomping.

Amelia must have interpreted this feeble sound as her asking for water, as Breanne felt a hand lift the back of her head, a water bottle placed to her lips. Blissful relief washed down her throat, the smooth, cool liquid the only pleasure she had remaining in life. All else was an agonising torture chamber of sensations she cursed and wished would cease. But none more so than that dreadful tapping of Jacub's pacing, driving her mad.

"Stop walking near my fucking head," she said, using up the few words she had at her disposal, her throat immediately constricting, feeling sore and dry once more. She smacked her lips. Amelia attentively pressed the bottle to them once more.

"Thank you," said Breanne, swallowing razor blades to do so.

"You're welcome, dear," said Amelia.

"It's my house. I'll walk where I want," said Jacub.

Amelia hissed at him in annoyance. Jacub angrily stomped in rebellious defiance, making his point at the expense of more agony for Breanne as the impacts reverberated through the floor and bounced around her fragile brain. The pain signals bundled up there and burst across her whole body in a wave which made her shudder involuntarily.

"Stop, you're hurting her," said Amelia.

"*I'm* hurting her? She went outside during a nuclear explosion. She nearly got us killed saving her, by the way, and what thanks do I get? I'm told I can't walk around in my own home."

"Go walk around the veranda."

"I'm not going out there," protested Jacub. "That cloud of fallout is hovering up in the stratosphere, but it'll have to come down sometime. It's an evil looking son of a bitch, too."

"Is that what you're saying is unnatural?"

"Heck no, woman, I'm talking about that second bleedin' sun!"

"It's just some type of optical illusion," said Amelia. "Something caused by the fallout cloud."

"No, it's not. It's moving about up there, following after the real one like some type of lovesick puppy. I'm telling you, two suns, it's not bloody natural!"

It is natural, thought Breanne. *It's the most natural thing in the world.*

She remembered seeing it when her consciousness left her body. It was an avatar of the Earth, a force unleashed to bring balance. But balance to what?

Unbidden, a word came to Breanne's mind, glowing there with the otherworldly light of radioactivity.

The word was Anathema.

34

"Here, it's time for you to take more painkillers, Jain," said Amelia from another room.

"No, give them to Breanne. She needs them more," said Jain.

She cares about me, thought Breanne, her heart beating hard in her chest. But it quickly dropped down into her stomach as the negative voice countered. *Or maybe she's a decent human, unlike me.*

"We're not wasting anything on that crazy bitch," shouted Jacub from halfway across the house, clearly wanting Breanne to hear as well. He continued to mutter to himself at a lower, yet still audible, level. "It's the damn end of the world, a nuclear holocaust, no less, and they think we've got medicine for everyone who busts in here."

"She's just a girl," Jain said to Amelia, and these words stung more than Jacub's, because Breanne didn't care what the old man thought, but Jain was a different matter entirely.

Why would she look twice at you, though, the state you're in? You're ugly, even uglier than before, thought Breanne, tears welling up in her eyes. *What am I doing here, among people who don't even care about me? But where are the people who do? Who are they? My parents abandoned me. Their work always comes first.*

"Their duty," she managed to spit with venom, as if the military was a person she hated, someone dragged her parents away from her against their will. And even though her mother had never been one to comfort her, she desperately wanted her to now, even if it was a forlorn hope and a total fantasy.

Amelia came into the room where they'd laid Breanne out on a bed.

"Are you alright, dear?" she asked.

Breanne shook her head. She felt the weight of the woman sink into the mattress by her thigh. It made her skin tingle at that spot, flaring into pain which spread out over her whole body. Breanne bit her lip.

"Does it hurt very badly?" asked Amelia, putting a hand on Breanne's shoulder.

Another nexus point of pain sprang into being at the touch, which, while kind, was ignorant and causing her discomfort through its presence.

"What do you care?" said Breanne, spittle on her lips.

Amelia wiped them with a moist towel. "I'm sorry about Jacub. He's scared, is all."

"Don't make excuses for him. He's an oaf."

"He's got a kind heart."

"Not towards me."

"You did punch him in the face."

"And you drew a knife on me," said Breanne, swatting away Amelia's hands.

"Yes, well, a lioness has to protect her family."

"Jain's not your family."

"Yes, she is. You don't know anything about us."

"I know more than you might think."

"What's that meant to mean?" asked Amelia, her body tensing, concern in her voice.

"I'm not stalking you," said Breanne, a little too hurriedly and defensively.

"You said you were worried about Marc and Jain, but I don't buy that."

"I do care about Jain!"

"But not Marc."

"Marc's dead."

Amelia gasped, and she grabbed Breanne on the shoulder, her fingers digging into the damaged skin.

Breanne yelped. Amelia leaned in close, the hot breath of her speech thrust into Breanne's ear.

"You couldn't possibly know that," she said.

"I've seen things. Let me go," wheedled Breanne, squirming.

"You're making shit up. God knows why. Jacub's right, you're crazy."

"She did know about Godrisaur," said Jain, her shuffling footsteps entering the room. Breanne heard her sigh heavily as she leant her weight against the bedhead.

"That's just a name she made up for it," said Amelia, getting up off the bed. "You shouldn't be up. Let me help you."

"No, it's a name Marc made up for it. Or at least that's what I thought, that he made it up himself. But how could Breanne know about it?"

"She's up to something. Maybe she and Marc know each other. She's not who she says she is."

"She's not saying she's anything," said Jain reasonably.

"I've never met Marc," said Breanne, shifting uncomfortably on the bed, feeling hampered by her lack of sight. She wanted to see the faces of the two women, get a read on them. She felt hamstrung in her ability to manipulate a conversation which could decide if she could stay or not.

And I'll die if they send me away. I'm blind. I can't look after myself. And it's a nuclear wasteland out there in the valley, probably in the village, too. For all I know my parents' house has been levelled. But if they send me away, I'll lose Jain, and what would be the point of living then?

"So how do you know the monster is called Godrisaur?" asked Jain.

"I have… I don't know… these visions. But I'm an artist, I see stuff in my mind," said Breanne.

"Marc is an artist. He's a writer."

"Was a writer," said Breanne, wanting Jain to hurry up and accept it so they could get on with the business of falling in love.

You don't deserve her.

"Fuck, I'm trying to throw you a bone here," said Jain harshly. "You could at least pretend like you're not a heartless cunt."

That doesn't sound good, thought Breanne.

"I'm sorry," she said.

"That's okay," said Jain, with an exasperated sigh. "Maybe you're a literal person."

She's a better person than I am, thought Breanne.

Jain said, "I don't know what Marc was going through these last few days, but he was experiencing some type of vision as well. It was like the monster was talking to him, that it was aware of his presence. In some ways, I think he thought he was creating the monster, which is crazy, I know."

Jain sat on the bed, laid a hand on Breanne's. For some reason it didn't cause pain in the way Amelia's touch did.

"But it's been a crazy time," continued Jain, "and nothing would surprise me anymore. It wasn't that long ago we were living a lovely life together, he and I, in our apartment in our quaint little town. Now there's a massive lizard stalking the valley and nuclear bombs going off. Our world is over, one way or another. Even if we live, nothing will ever be the same again."

"As long as we're together," said Breanne and she was relieved that Jain didn't pull away in disgust. She heard Amelia make a huffing noise of disapproval nearby, but she ignored this, engrossed in Jain's intoxicating presence.

"I want Marc back," said Jain. "I have a feeling you can help me, Breanne. Will you help me?"

"I'll do anything for you," said Breanne.

But Marc is definitely already dead.

"Good, good," said Jain softly. She got up and said to Amelia in a much more utilitarian tone, "Give her the painkillers."

Then she left.

35

The painkillers gave Breanne some relief from the dark coffin of agony in which she existed. Her reality dissolved into an infinite space of non-sight, her consciousness drifting around in it, with little in the way of external stimuli or sensation to ground her. The drugs played a tune on the sparkling darkness which had replaced her vision, and each note was seen rather than heard, a splash of colour like paint on a canvas.

It was only as she watched these that it started to dawn on her that she might be blind forever, never able to paint again with a physical brush and canvas. She'd grow old with only fading memories of sight and beauty glimpsed in the miasma of her mind.

Though this should upset her, she was too numb to cry. Her thoughts drifted away from the emotional pain, drawn like a moth to another light. It was a ball of brilliance, with a sharp, stabbing corona of fiery tendrils licking around its surface. It floated in her mind's eye like a sun, almost too bright to look at. Even her second sight seemed to slide off it, as if it couldn't lock on to its location for long, or perhaps its form was amorphous and constantly changing, its transmogrification hidden from regular vision by its intense luminosity. It was a chameleon, its cloak changing colour depending on who viewed it and from how far away. From a distant galaxy it probably looked red, or blue, or white. Perhaps it sparkled, twinkling between many colours in quick succession. But to Breanne, chasing after it, her etheric body floating on nothingness, it looked yellow, and the colours it did not keep for itself were projected outwards onto other objects.

Breanne caught a glimpse of these many colours, this rainbow patina like a shifting oil slick. Turning her head which was not a head, she saw wings which were not wings. They melded and morphed like a hallucination, bending and folding in on themselves, expanding and contracting, taking on fresh shapes each second. They were fuzzy in their formlessness, hazy in their lack of solidity, furry with fine hairs which blew in an unfelt breeze, each a different colour. There were more colours here than had ever existed with the poor excuse for eyes she'd been born with, now lost and replaced by multifaceted ones which saw many realities from many different perspectives. They allowed her to see what she had become, or would become, once she emerged from this cocoon of darkness in which she found herself in her waking world.

To witness the majesty of this creature—which both was and wasn't herself—Breanne felt a fresh hope that the art she wished to express wasn't lost to her. If only she could see again, she would attempt to paint this giant moth she was becoming, which was becoming her, as it endlessly chased after a sun it couldn't catch yet wanted to.

Wanting, always wanting—drawn by desire and frustration the moth chased the flame.

I just want to be free, thought Breanne, and she knew, deep in her soul, this was the one thing she was not, and never could be.

We're lured on by promises of hope, by the lies of the Anathema.

36

Aided by the painkillers, Breanne slept deeply. Lost in a murky pool of unconsciousness, it was only with sludgy reluctance that she began to rise back towards the world of wakefulness. Despite the clinging tendrils of slumber, wrapped around her ankles and holding her down, she was drawn upwards by a siren's song. It swirled around her with naked suggestiveness, tantalising her ears with promises of what might be. Above her was a shimmering light which hovered somewhere beyond the broken and choppy surface of sleep, like the sun seen through the shifting lens of the ocean's currents.

"Breanne, wake up," said a voice. It sounded muffled, blocked by the water, and she thought it must be the light beckoning her. There were unspoken secrets in that voice, which made Breanne wary, but it was hard not to be drawn on by the equally unspoken potential of it. There was love there—of a type—and it was being offered to her, if only she could pay the price it demanded.

This was enough to send her rushing towards the surface, almost panicking, not wanting to miss out on everything she had ever wanted: acceptance, love, compassion, companionship. She rocked back and forth as she ascended, feeling the push and pull of the water's current around her, like many hands tugging this way and that. They wanted something in return for what they offered, but their expectations changed each moment, so Breanne had no idea what she was signing up for, and knew only that she was now committed.

"Hey, wake up," said the voice again, hooking her like a fish and dragging her out of the water with its violent insistence.

Reality smashed over Breanne's head like a pane of shattering glass, harsh and sudden.

"I don't know what you want from me!" she shrieked and gulped down air as if she'd been drowning, which in her experience was a good estimation of what it was like to wake up having a panic attack.

"I want you to shut the fuck up. You'll wake Marc's parents," hissed Jain, grabbing Breanne by the shoulders and shoving her hard back onto the bed. When Breanne still wouldn't stop floundering or making confused moaning sounds, Jain jumped on top of her and held her down, one hand over her mouth.

The crushing weight on top of her, plus the restriction on her breathing, made Breanne feel like she was buried alive. The panic attack worsened. She panted hard through her nostrils and bucked her hips at Jain, who responded by pushing her own down hard to force her to stop.

A shot of electricity passed through this point of contact, ramming through Breanne's body like a revelation. Her brain came to life with the sparkling explosions of previously untapped neuron pathways opening up. It was an overwhelming sensation which short-circuited the panic attack, and Breanne slumped on the bed, exhausted, her blind eyes darting back and forth, searching for but not finding an explanation for what had just happened to her.

Jain slid her hand away slowly—ready to clamp it back down again—and then her body with it, slithering free like a slippery-skinned snake.

"Get up and get dressed," she said.

Breanne didn't respond right away, still trying to catch her breath, still trying to process—and perhaps savour—the surreal and extreme polarity of the experience she'd had. It was burned hard into her brain, and she could recall it all, at least she thought she could. But the true sensations of it faded, never quite captured again, existing only as echoes and shadows of the thing, haunting the recesses of her mind in the future.

"Did you hear me?" asked Jain. Breanne could hear her scrabbling around in a closet.

"Yes," she responded, confused. "But why? And I have no clothes. They were torn to shreds by the blasts."

"You and Marc are about the same size."

Breanne felt clothing tossed onto her. The fabric felt rough against her burns and wounds, even the softest cloth harsh and abrasive.

"You want me to wear your dead boyfriend's clothes?" said Breanne.

"Don't you fucking say that word again, alright? He's not... *that*," said Jain, her tone turning between harsh and soft on a dime, alternating with her wildly fluctuating emotions, barely under control. "And what's wrong with his clothes? Not feminine enough for you? I saw your style. Not exactly a cocktail dress, heels, and a purse."

"But—"

"Look, we're going to find him."

"If you say so," said Breanne, sick of arguing already, sad that the magic of the moment was gone so suddenly. Now the pain was back. She weakly pulled herself upright and pawed at the clothes.

"Yes, I do say so," said Jain. "I know you can see things other people can't. You're going to help me find Marc."

Breanne made a face, rolled her eyes. Jain must have seen this as she said, "I'm not crazy. Are *you* crazy?"

"I could be. I'm experiencing things I've never experienced before, both externally and internally, and I wasn't exactly normal to begin with."

"Well," Jain said, not unkindly, "life is more than a little crazy right now, giant Kaiju attack and nuclear bombs. I suppose one more piece of insanity in the mix can hardly hurt."

"I don't like being referred to as one more piece of insanity."

"Not you, just, I don't know... *whatever it is* that you and Marc share, the second sight, or some other voodoo shit."

"It's not going to bring him back. I can see things—"

"You're blind."

"Is that a joke?"

"Yes."

I can't believe she just said that, thought Breanne, but she pretended like it didn't offend her, and continued, "I can see things, but not influence them. I'm not creating anything."

"You didn't paint any pictures of Godrisaur, make any art about it?"

"No."

"But you know its name, and other things besides, I'm sure."

"I know more than I'd like."

"Like what?"

"That Godrisaur ate your boyfriend."

There was silence for a long time.

"It doesn't mean anything," said Jain eventually, "because I've got a plan to save him."

"One that involves me," said Breanne.

"Yes."

"You know I'm really hurt, right?"

"Oh, and I'm just skipping happy with this leg wound I got. It's a real blast."

"Is that a nuclear explosion joke?"

"No, it is not."

"You're weird," said Breanne.

"That makes two of us."

This made Breanne smile, and she felt Jain smile too, a softening of the tension in the air.

"I'm sorry to put you through this," said Jain.

"It's okay, but I need you to help me with these clothes," said Breanne, already wincing at the thought of them rubbing against her raw skin. "And do you have any more of those painkillers?"

37

"Okay," said Jain, "let's do this."

She guided Breanne through the house, taking a series of turns, culminating in the opening of a squeaking door, which Jain shushed.

"Why are we being quiet?" asked Breanne.

Jain gave her a tug on the elbow. "Watch the step down. I told you, Marc's parents are sleeping."

"Is it night time?"

"Yeah."

"Why don't we wait for the morning?"

"We're stealing their car," said Jain, shuffling them forward together. "And what do you care? You can't see anyway."

"I would have thought *you'd* want to see, at the very least."

"I've got a torch, one of those big chunky Dolphin ones that float."

"If you have that, why are Amelia and Jacub getting around using candles?" said Breanne, then, pre-empting the obvious question, added, "I smelled the burning wax."

"If you hadn't noticed, they're a little bit eccentric."

"You should meet my parents."

"They're like you?"

"Not at all."

"You think they're alright?" asked Jain. The question was one of curiosity, not designed to hurt, but it hurt Breanne because she felt she knew the answer. "They're alive, if that's what you mean. At least I think so. Are they alright, though? I'm guessing no."

"What makes you say that?"

"My dad was one of the pilots who dropped the bombs."

"Whoa, that's heavy. You think he knew you were down here?"

"I'm house sitting for them down the road. So, yeah, I suppose he did."

Jain scoffed. "You're making this up. They wouldn't tell you about that."

"The military?"

"Your parents."

"Same thing," said Breanne, her voice strained with pain. "But no, they didn't tell me. They never tell me anything. I saw it in the same way I see everything now—in my mind."

"And you think that makes it true? It's hard to believe he'd do that to his own daughter."

"It's the only reality I've got now."

"You're blind, Breanne, not dead. You're still a person. There's no need to retreat into your own fantasy world."

"Yes, there is," said Breanne seriously. "Because it's the only way you'll ever see Marc again."

And it's the only place you and I will ever be together, she thought.

38

"What type of car are we stealing?" asked Breanne. She tried to guess by the sound of the door opening and the feel of the seat Jain plonked her down into, but quickly realised her knowledge of cars was inadequate to use these meagre clues.

"It's an X-type Jaguar," said Jain.

"Is that some type of cool sports car?"

"Yeah, but only if you're an old person buying yourself a retirement present twenty years ago. Wait there."

"Where am I going to go?"

"Just shut up. I'll open the garage door. This might be loud enough to wake them up."

"You would have thought our talking would have woken them already."

"They're partially deaf and heavy sleepers," said Jain. "But they have some type of sixth sense about people messing with their stuff, so I bet Jacub will be out here in moments now we've touched his car."

The garage door made an unholy racket, the metal screeching torturously as Jain hauled it up.

"I don't think they need a sixth sense for that one," said Breanne, fumbling in the air until she got hold of the handle, and pulled the door shut. Jain got in on the other side in a flash, starting the car. It revved throatily as she pumped the gas.

"Got a good roar on it," said Jain, adding after a pause, "Godrisaur joke."

"They're always funnier when you have to say it's a joke."

Jain shifted it into reverse. "Marc would have laughed."

39

"I think they slept through that racket," said Breanne as they zoomed down the driveway and along the street, past the rock walls that skirted the house.

"No, I'm sure they're up and cursing us out roundly," said Jain.

"Probably blaming me, think I've kidnapped you or something."

"They don't like you, no, but that's a stretch. At least they're rid of you."

"You too."

"What? They love me. I'm family."

"Marc's their family. And they didn't even go looking for him."

"That's harsh. They're old people and they're scared. I mean, look at the state of their village!"

"Maybe you can describe it."

"Oh, yeah, sorry. It's a fucking mess, rocks and debris everywhere. Whole houses smashed to bits. Some are on fire."

There was a jolt as the car ran over something.

"What was that?" asked Breanne.

"Dead body. At least I *hope* they are already dead."

"Do you want to go back and check?"

"No, I don't," said Jain. They zigzagged left and right. "There's plenty more corpses on the road, don't you worry about that. And the still-living people I can see don't look much better. God, they look like, umm…" She trailed off.

"Like what?"

"Ah, nothing."

"Like me," said Breanne. "Burnt, mutilated."

Jain pretended she didn't hear. "I don't know what they're doing, just shuffling around like zombies."

"So I look like a zombie. Great, thanks."

"That's not what I said."

Breanne started to cry. "No one's ever going to love me."

"Stop that. That's not true."

"It doesn't even matter. We're all going to die anyway."

"We'll get through this," Jain said with stoic confidence.

"You've obviously forgotten about the fallout."

"Bit hard to. The night sky shimmers with it. Looks like an oil slick."

"It's a warning, like the bright colours on a poisonous frog."

"I worked in hospitals, I know about radiation sickness," said Jain, though she didn't sound as confident anymore.

"So you know we're fucked."

"That was going to fuck us whether we stayed in the house or not. It'll get in the food, in the water."

Breanne sniffled. "Better chance sheltered indoors."

"No, our only chance is out here. We need to take control of our destiny."

"And how the hell are we going to do that? What in the fuck are we even doing out here, driving around in a post-apocalyptic wasteland?"

"We're going to rewrite the story," said Jain.

40

"In some ways you do a pretty good job of passing as normal," Breanne said, "but you're as weird as the rest of us."

"What even *is* normal?" asked Jain, grunting with annoyance as she swerved the car around obstacles. "We're all mentally ill somehow. To be human is to be mentally ill. Trust me, I studied dementia. A lot can go wrong with the human brain."

"Plus, you date a writer, they're weird as. I guess you pass as less weird in comparison."

"We're not dating. We're in love. I'll love him forever, no matter what happens. We're life partners."

Breanne felt her heart sink, splashing into her guts like nausea. "Must be nice, to be so in love, willing to risk your life for him, even when you know the odds are so slim."

"I have to admit, what we're doing is a bit of a longshot."

"So, what's this grand plan?"

"Well, at first I thought we'd go find Marc, of course, which meant heading towards Godrisaur. But the closer we get the more I realise that's hopeless. The monster is nothing but a tumbled ruin of rocks."

"What time is it?"

"The sun's coming up on the horizon."

"Well, whatever your revised plan is," said Breanne, "I suggest you hurry up, because that pile of smouldering rocks isn't the monster anymore. And whatever it's become, it's coming back."

"What it's become?"

"That second sun Jacub was talking about."

"Yeah, I saw it. Freaky fucking thing."

"That's Godrisaur, its essence, at least. I've seen it in my mind. Though the giant volcanic lizard is dead, it's transforming into something else now, and I don't think it's going to suddenly become benevolent towards humanity. So, whatever mad quest we're on, I think you should get a wriggle on."

"Easier said than done," said Jain, revving the engine. Breanne was pushed back into her chair by the acceleration. She was thrown forward again painfully as Jain stomped the brakes, the car fishtailing through an S-shaped turn. "There's a fuck tonne of Godrisaur pieces scattered everywhere."

"Where are we going?" asked Breanne.

"I'm trying to get through to where I think I'll find it, but the roads are blocked in places and I've had to try new ways I'm not familiar with. Then there's the water from the tsunami, though that's slowly starting to drain away, revealing other options."

"Find it? Find *what*?"

Breanne could hear Jain tense up in the creaky leather seat, as if she knew what she was about to say was going to sound deranged. When she said it, there was a weird inflection at the end of the sentence, as if she were asking a question, or testing Breanne's reaction.

"We're going to find Marc's laptop?"

41

"A *fucking laptop!*" shrieked Breanne, surprising herself with the volume. Jain flinched, the car jinking to the side in sympathetic unity.

"Don't yell at me," said Jain with a sob, immediately on the verge of tears.

Breanne didn't lower her voice, becoming even shriller. "Well, what is it, a *fucking magic laptop*?"

"It's Marc's laptop," Jain said lamely, as if that explained it.

Breanne ran her hand through her hair in annoyance, and tried to take a deep breath. When her hand came away with a clump of her hair in it, she lost it all over again, screaming incoherent curses at Jain, at Godrisaur, at her father, at the bombs, at the miserable wreck of her life.

"You done?" asked Jain tersely when there was a break.

Breanne panted. "Oh, I'm done alright. We're both done. Well done, like a hunk of chargrilled meat, me physically, and you in the head. You're fucking cooked, Jain."

"Marc seemed to think what he wrote on that computer changed reality, brought Godrisaur to life and influenced its actions." Jain sounded much calmer and saner than Breanne thought she had any right to.

Though, who am I to judge, thought Breanne, *given the things I've seen in my mind?*

"We're all nuts," she said out loud.

"Yeah, trust me, I know," said Jain, laughter in her voice.

Breanne's heart melted to hear that bubbly joy. She could picture Jain's beautiful smile, her teeth flashing in happiness.

Will I ever see it again?

"Marc would have liked you, you know," said Jain.

That might be so, but I hate him, because he's dead and yet he's still got you, thought Breanne.

"I wanted to be a writer," she said instead.

"Oh, really? As well as painting?"

"Yeah, but I'm dyslexic."

"You can overcome that," said Jain with pragmatic certainty. "Amelia's dyslexic. She still writes children's stories. I've read a few. They're fun. She was a teacher before she retired."

"They're a family of writers," Breanne said glumly.

"Not Jacub! He reads, though. Big books."

Breanne's response was monotone and automatic, drifting into small talk. "He must be really into reading."

"Not as much as he likes a bargain. Big books mean more pages for your money." Jain laughed.

Breanne chuckled weakly along with her. She felt a gap developing, a chasm between them, with Jain and Marc's family on one side, and her, a lone freak, on the other, not a part of that solid, cohesive unit.

42

There was a ravine stretching out ahead of them, blocking their progress, or perhaps marking their destination. Breanne couldn't see it, but as Jain helped her from the parked car, led her to the edge, she could feel it like a yawning abyss before her. A sense of unreasoning vertigo overcame her, which should have been absent along with her sight. It tugged at her like the wind tugged at her clothes, dragging her forward, willing her to jump into that vast open space. Her foot skittered forward on some rocks and she almost went over, but a hand held her back. It belonged to Jain. She was the only thing keeping Breanne upright, and she wasn't so steady on her feet either, favouring her good leg.

"You alright?" asked Breanne.

"Yeah, but my leg hurts like a bastard." Jain hopped around on the spot, trying to get more comfortable. Breanne planted her feet more firmly to give her something more reliable to lean on, despite the pain it caused.

"Thanks," said Jain.

Breanne took in a bracing lungful of air. It tickled her nostrils. "Smells like ash here."

"Used to be a forest, but now it's just charred stumps. Godrisaur burned it down with that… I don't know what you'd call it."

"The light beam, the one it shot from its mouth?"

"Yeah, you saw that?"

"I was watching through my father's telescope when it burned down a wooded area further down the ridge from the village."

"Really? That's where we are! The road leads up to the cliff here by your feet."

Breanne probed around curiously with a foot, causing the two of them to sway.

"Yeah, careful, you nearly went over before," said Jain, flailing her arms for balance. "Damn, you'll take me with you. I'm not so solid on my feet at the moment."

"Why'd you bring me here?" asked Breanne, looking around despite being blind, catching flickers of light in the peripheries of what had once been her line of sight. She chased them down with jerks of her head but they fled from her like ghosts that didn't want to be seen.

"Because I think this is where Marc lost his laptop," said Jain. "We had a bag with some things in it. He dumped the contents and used it to bandage my leg. I don't know where exactly, but around here somewhere. Maybe that stuff burned in the fire."

"And the laptop with it."

"Maybe," Jain repeated, letting go of Breanne. She could be heard sifting through the ashes with a stick. "If it was here, it'd be ruined, but it'd still be here."

"It could be anywhere."

"No, Marc still had it in his jacket on the other side."

"Other side?"

"Of this ravine. I sometimes forget you can't see anything. Must be frustrating. The road used to run over a bridge which spanned across this gap between two cliffs, with a highway running through down below. It was covered by water last time we were here but that's mostly gone now."

"And you think the laptop is, what, on the other cliff? Good luck climbing it."

"I'm hoping not, but no. He wouldn't have left it there, not then, not before…" Jain trailed off, and Breanne could hear her breathing heavily. Breanne held out her hand, felt Jain's flapping around wildly like a startled bird. She gripped it, and it calmed a touch, settling snuggly into her palm.

"Down there—" said Jain, but didn't say anymore, her words pinching off as her throat choked closed audibly.

Breanne looked down, not expecting to see anything, of course, but gasped when she found there was indeed something for her to see. It was a faint glowing outline at first, but the more she fixated on it the more definition it gained. Gossamer light played around it, filling in more details. It was a man, a green ghost. He was sitting, hunched over, staring down at another glowing shape, this one red.

"He's dead," Breanne said.

Jain gasped, squeezed her hand hard. "You can see that?"

"The ghost? Yeah."

"You can see *ghosts*?"

"What are you looking at then?"

"A dead body. It's in the boat down there at the base of the cliff."

Breanne focused on the red shape, saw that it was a man, an inert corpse drawn in glowing spectral blood. There was a black spike jutting from his back, a blade made out of shadow. The green ghost inspected it wistfully, as if wishing things had turned out differently.

"We didn't want to… you know," said Jain, pumping Breanne's hand and tugging at it with her own, as if imploring her to believe her. "But he attacked us."

Breanne watched the green ghost, also a man. He was reaching for the shadow blade, but each time he got close he pulled back as if the blade was scorching hot. Frowning, the green ghost went on inspecting the body. Breanne realised both spectral forms were of the same man, like a prism had split the ghost into two refractions, a green and a red.

"You have to go down there and pull that knife out of his back," she said to Jain, who responded with a sharp intake of breath like heated metal thrust into water.

"Woof, no, thanks," said Jain. "That's some pretty morbid shit. And how would I even get down there with my leg?"

"With great difficulty?" suggested Breanne.

"No kidding."

"You have to do it, though. He's suffering."

"Who? The dead guy?"

"Yeah."

"He's dead!" protested Jain.

"His soul is stuck here on this plane. I think he was surprised to be murdered—"

"That's an ugly word."

"It's an accurate word."

"Look, we didn't have a choice!" said Jain, pulling away her hand, her voice rising hysterically. "The guy was nuts. He wanted my necklace as payment to take us across the floodwaters in his boat. I mean, Marc gave me that for my birthday, and he just took it!"

Jain's voice moved around in tightly paced circles.

"That was bad enough," she continued, "but his dog tried to bite Marc, and Marc pushed it overboard. We couldn't find the dog, the current was so strong. The guy lost his head and came at me with a knife."

Breanne was watching it vividly re-enacted, either in her imagination or by the ghostly green shape, she couldn't quite tell which. The scene played over and over again in a closed loop of ghostly silhouettes, echoes of the past. It made her blood boil to think of Jain in such danger.

"And so Marc hit him over the head with this little wooden club you bash fish with," said Jain, tapping Breanne on the skull with her fist, miming the action. "When he went down, Marc stabbed him with the knife."

I never thought I'd say this, but good on you, Marc, thought Breanne.

Jain was breathing heavily, as if she'd made a confession to the police and expected to be carted off to jail. But after the nuclear blasts the East Coast of Australia was a post-apocalyptic ruin, with no law, no order, and no one was coming to judge her.

Except the dead.

The ghost was staring up imploringly at them.

"He wants you to end this," said Breanne.

"Why me?" said Jain, the confession over as suddenly as it began. She was back on the defensive. Breanne didn't say anything, raising her eyebrows.

"Okay, okay," said Jain after a pause. "I might have given him a kick around the head for good measure."

Breanne waited. So did the ghost.

"Then I spat on him, alright?" said Jain. "But that's it." She clapped her hands, dusting them off as this was the final word. Breanne looked down at the ghost—who shook his head slowly—and then back in the direction of Jain's heavy breathing.

"Fuck, fuck, fuck," muttered Jain, hobbling around in agitation. "Look, I might of... you know, told Marc to finish him off, but I didn't *murder* the guy. It was self-defence."

"That's heavy," said Breanne.

"Oh, shut up."

"I'm not judging you. I'm saying that it's plain to see—to me, at least—that this is something you have to do. I'd hurry, too, if I were you. You said the sun's coming up, right?"

"Yeah, what's that got to do with it?"

"Well, the monster, that second sun, will be hot on its heels in the sky. I for one don't want to be out here when it flies overhead."

"Ugh!" said Jain, slapping her flanks in resignation. "Go and check in the boot of the car, see if there's a piece of rope or a fucking towline or some shit."

Breanne turned her blind gaze in the direction of the voice, giving Jain a deadpan look.

"Oh," said Jain. "Right."

43

"Fuck, fuck, fuck," said Jain, audibly straining and struggling as she descended the cliff. "Fuck this shit."

There hadn't been any rope in the car, but there had been tough straps for tying things to a roof rack, which Jain had remarked was ironic, as the Jaguar didn't have a roof rack.

"Seems like a Jacub thing to have in the car, though," she'd said with a knowing laugh. "You know, just in case."

The straps weren't long enough to reach all the way down the cliff, or even a good portion of it. Instead, they'd alighted upon a plan. With the straps tied together end to end, Jain looped them over a rock like a sling, giving it a test tug to see if it held. Then she lowered herself a few metres—awkward with her bad leg—onto a ledge or rock. Pulling the straps down by tugging on one end, she found another anchor point and repeated the process. It was slow going.

"Shit, shit, shit on a biscuit," said Jain, accompanied by the sound of rocks falling.

"Are you alright?" asked Breanne, who had found a perch on the edge to sit on and wasn't going to move an inch until Jain returned, afraid of falling.

If Jain doesn't fall to her death herself, she thought, feeling helpless, hating being blind all over again.

"Yeah, knocking a lot of rocks loose though," said Jain. One banged with a thud against the hull of the boat. Breanne looked down, saw the green ghost dancing around as if dodging the rocks, or fretting over them hitting his corpse.

"Be careful," she said. "The ghost doesn't like that."

"Fuck the ghost. I'm not doing it on purpose," said Jain with a grunt of effort, dislodging more rocks.

Breanne willed her on, fear gathering in her heart as an unspoken tension built in the air. She felt a looming weight, the hair on the back of her neck standing up, as if a hammer was being held aloft over the back of her skull, ready to strike down at any moment.

"Could you hurry it up a bit?" she shouted down the cliff.

Jain snorted. "Be careful, she says, but hurry it up, won't you? Make up your damn mind, woman."

A flash drew Breanne's second sight up towards the level of the horizon. There was a spot of light there, already much bigger and brighter than the ghost, and far more terrifying.

"Uh, I think you should lean towards hurrying up, if at all possible," she said, the fear she'd been feeling finding something to lock onto like a beacon lit in the dark shadows of her soul.

"Yeah, because that's totally possible with this damned leg," Jain said sarcastically, though the sounds of her movement did gain more urgency.

Breanne kept her eyes locked on this new light. It sparkled in the darkness of her ruined vision, a burning ball which grew in size each second, trailing a million specks of light like embers from a fire.

"Godrisaur…" she breathed in hushed awe, but even as she said it she knew the name was wrong. This thing, this monster, was Godrisaur no longer. What she was witnessing was the dawn of a new creature, not yet born, but coalescing around the furnace star which had laid at the heart of the giant lizard, released upon its destruction by the nuclear blasts. Now set free, it was regenerating, undergoing a process of physical reincarnation into whatever horrific form it would take on next.

And Breanne suspected she knew what it was becoming. She'd seen it in her mind. Hauntingly beautiful, with kaleidoscope patterns changing across its body, it was a vision of mutation and change.

It was Death given flight, swooping across the land in the wake of its enemy, the sun, desperate for vengeance, but still weak, building its power. It needed fuel. It needed to eat life.

"Those embers," said Breanne, feeling the corresponding spark inside her being tugged at, hungered for.

The beast rushed across the sky and Breanne quaked.

It was coming to consume their souls.

44

From the base of the cliff, Breanne heard the sliding of feet through a rocky scree, terminating in a thump. A stream of invective bubbled up from Jain, followed by a weary, "Okay, I'm down."

"Did you fall into the boat?" asked Breanne, calling down to her with a hand cupped to her mouth. Jain didn't answer except for more muttered cursing.

Breanne looked back to the horizon, trying to gauge how much time they had. The ball of light—the energy core of the monster—swelled in size as it approached. It trailed after a sun whose illumination Breanne was blind to, though she could taste its energetic signature. It was the black mirror of the monster, pushing aside the sparkling darkness of her dead eyes with its powerful bow wave as it marched across the heavens like a stately God.

Breanne felt helpless, utterly small and insignificant. They were in the middle of a cosmic confrontation so huge it twisted her mind to contemplate its scope. She felt betrayed by reality itself.

I've been lied to my whole life, she thought. *What is the true nature of the sun if some monster so desperately wants to do battle with it?*

She had no idea what they were up against, and indeed if there was anything they could do to stop it.

Stop it?

She scoffed at her hubris.

Impossible—we're simply going to be crushed between the unbearable weight of this new reality, our small lives snuffed out as two unfathomably large forces clash.

She jumped to her feet, wanting to do something, but immediately she was out of her depth. Her sense of centre was hopelessly out of whack in all respects, and she swayed on her feet, nearly tumbling over the edge of the cliff.

You're going to get yourself killed.

She promptly plonked her ass back down, her burned skin protesting at the contact with the rocks beneath her, at the abrasive clothes which rubbed like sandpaper. It cruelly reminded her of her condition, the desperate nature of her plight.

You're already dead.

The pain flared across the entire canvas of her skin as panic built.

But is that really the end?

She glanced back down at the ghost. The man fretted his spectral hands, his glowing features twisting in consternation. He nodded at the light in the sky, then down at his former body.

"Okay, I've got you," she said to him under her breath, and yelled at Jain, "Pull the dagger out."

"What? Are you nuts? I'm looking for the laptop," said Jain, hissing in pain as she hopped about the fibreglass hull of the boat.

"You've got to do this first."

"I don't know why I have to do it at all," said Jain distractedly, engrossed in her search of the boat. Breanne heard hatches and cabinets thrown open and slammed shut, boxes of fishing tackle dumped out with metallic clinks. "Ouch, that's a tetanus shot."

"We've got to get out of here!" said Breanne, making her fear and urgency plain. It was mirrored by the ghost, who was beside himself in his desire to escape.

"I'm not going without the laptop."

"You've still got to get back up the cliff somehow."

"It'll be easier coming up. I can use my arms more."

Breanne looked at the burning ball of energy in the sky. The trail of etheric sparks it dragged in its wake was getting weightier by the moment, more points of light joining it, shooting up from the Earth like moths to a flame.

"If you don't get that dagger out, this guy's soul is going to get sucked up by the monster," she said.

"Good," said Jain. "He deserves it."

"There's a good chance it'll happen to us, too, if we die out here."

"I'm not planning on dying out here, are you?"

Breanne felt a goad of terror stab the base of her brain. "No, so do as I say and pull the damn dagger out!"

"Fine, if it'll shut you up."

Breanne watched as the ghostly man hovered over his gory corpse light. With a suddenness she wasn't expecting, the dark blade ripped free of the red body, which melted and spread like a pool of blood, then evaporated into a dissipating mist. She expected the green figure of the man to do the same, but instead he turned his head up, smiled at Breanne. He opened the ghostly jacket he wore, pulled an object from it. It was a laptop. He handed it to someone offstage of the spectral stage he trod. It disappeared from Breanne's sight.

"Hey, the laptop just popped out of nowhere into my bloody hands!" shouted Jain in utter astonishment.

Breanne and the ghost shared a laugh, but then his face set grim. He turned his back on her and on the physical world, and shot upwards, as if the chain anchoring him to this life had been severed. He was heading towards the surface of a new life, a new reality.

But the monster loomed in the sky now, close and hot like a noonday sun. And Breanne felt the heat of it like a scalding brand on her burned skin. She screamed in terror, both for herself and to see the fate which awaited them all in death.

We were too late for him, she thought as the man's soul soared high, free for only a moment. He tried to get beyond the grasping tendrils of the monster's light, to escape into the void of nothingness where he could rest in peace. Instead, he was consumed in fire as they reached for him like fiery whips. His scream was silent as he was consumed, burning like a wisp of paper in a flame, becoming nothing more than sparkling embers which disappeared into the great mass of burning souls, dragged along by the weighty gravity of the passing monster.

And he wasn't alone. The dead from all across the region were being sucked up, a glittering cascade of broken shards of glass, catching the light of the sun as they fell in reverse. In their reflection, Breanne caught glimmers of what might have been, of lives that had been stolen, cut short, snuffed out. She saw her own life there, the one where she was whole, with all her senses, and not mutilated. It was a reality where Jain and she could be together, cruelly stolen by the greed of an entity she did not understand yet hated all the same.

And she knew which name to curse now. As the monster tore overhead, it screamed a silent word only those linked to it by some ephemeral cord could hear. Breanne was dismayed to realise she was one of those to receive this dark blessing. It was why she could still see it despite being blind. She was being invited into the realm of the next monster, the one yet to be born. She opened her mouth, echoing the monster's scream with her own as she shouted its name into the sky.

"Mothzen!"

45

The monster's burning core rained fire as it flew overhead. Breanne could smell the smoke and feel the heat of the falling fireballs. She could hear Jain screaming, as well as many others, the desperate cry of thousands of humans all over the hills and ridges of the area. The combined note of their terror quavered on the air, undulating like a mourning wail.

Their grief is justified, thought Breanne. *Here is the harbinger of our doom.*

Where the burning fireballs struck the ground they exploded with spectral light which Breanne could see, the explosions looking like twinkling stars in the night sky to her dark vision. Death followed for the people of the valley, the killing indiscriminate, awful agony universal. The monster's powerful wake tore the souls from the charred corpses and dragged them along behind it.

It's fuelling its ascension, thought Breanne, *gathering resources for the transformation.*

"Help me!" shouted Jain from nearby. Breanne was shocked she was so close.

"You really did climb back up faster than you went down," she said, reaching out blindly with one hand and anchoring her weight by holding onto a rock with the other. Jain's fingers brushed against hers, an electrifying caress, and for a second, Breanne forgot her fear, engrossed in another strong emotion.

"It's easy to get a move on when there's a firestorm falling from the sky," said Jain, panting hard. "Can you hold your hand still?"

Breanne did so, and Jain's hand slid into hers so perfectly it was like a key entering a lock.

We're made for each other.

Jain dragged her whole weight up by the grip. It nearly took Breanne over the edge.

At least we'd both die together.

Next thing she knew, Breanne was being helped to her feet in turn by Jain. They hobbled quickly to the car like a single lame, blind donkey. Jain threw open a door and shoved Breanne rudely across the backseat, slamming the door to silence her cry of protest. She got in the front and Breanne told her off with renewed vehemence as she struggled to get the right way up, her head down in the foot well.

"You think I give a fuck right now?" said Jain, starting the engine and grinding the gearstick with an ugly sound. "If you don't like the seating arrangements, I can drop you off at the next bus stop."

"I'm pretty sure the buses are out of service," said Breanne sarcastically, righting herself with some effort. She fumbled around for the seatbelt, which was hard to find and fasten with Jain reversing hard. She got it clipped in place just in time as Jain threw the car into a g-force spin with the screech of a pulled handbrake which jolted Breanne around painfully.

"You should have been a stunt driver," she said.

"And you should have been a smart ass. Wait, too late, you're already a pro," said Jain through gritted teeth, the engine revving like a wild beast as she pushed the car as hard as she could down the ridge road.

"You got the laptop?" Sweat poured across Breanne's skin. It was getting hot in the car, the fireballs whooshing by outside. Those landing closest peppered the car door with burning debris. The air was bitter to taste.

"Of course I got the laptop. I wasn't leaving without it."

"I saw the ghost take it out of his jacket."

The slap of a palm against Jain's head was audible, her sarcasm dripping. "So *that's* where it was hiding, inside of a bloody ghost! Of course, why didn't *I* think of that?"

"He needed his due. I guess he felt ripped off that you stole back your necklace."

"Stole? It was mine all along."

"Still, you've got to pay the ferryman to take you across the river."

"Well, he's across the River Styx now," said Jain. "And he can stay there and burn in hell. Though, by the looks of it, we're in for a taste of that too."

Breanne reached out, touched the glass of the car window. She pulled it away—it was hot.

"I think he's in a place very much like hell," she said to distract herself from their desperate situation. "He got drawn into the burning heart of the monster. It's using their souls to power its transformation into a new form, gathering them about it like a fiery cocoon."

"That sounds like a fate worse than death," said Jain.

"And it's what happened to Marc, if he's anywhere."

The car screeched to a halt, Jain turning to scream in Breanne's face, covering it with spittle. "And why the fuck would you say a thing like that?"

Breanne's mouth moved mutely, trying to think of something, but Jain wasn't waiting for a response. She threw the sports car back into gear and sped off, swerving and jinking wildly around obstacles and falling fireballs without slowing.

She doesn't love me, thought Breanne. *Even if Marc is truly gone, she'll go on loving him forever. I can't replace him. Not unless I make her forget, and there's no way I can do that, is there?*

"You wanted the laptop so we can retell the story, didn't you?" she asked Jain, who grunted in assent.

Breanne continued, "Then even if he's inside the monster, we can get him out."

Or bury him so deep no one remembers his name.

46

They didn't speak again until Jain finally slowed the Jaguar a touch, which Breanne took to mean they were entering the village. The fireballs fell here with even greater intensity, the monster's immolating core passing directly overhead.

"Do you think we can stop at my parents' house, maybe get me some of my own clothes?" Breanne asked.

"It's up here on the left, isn't it?" said Jain. "Just before Elsa's house?"

"Yeah."

"Out of luck, *sorry*. It got crushed by a giant piece of Godrisaur's rocky ass."

Breanne didn't know if she was serious or not, but Jain continued with obvious dark relish. "Completely flattened, smashed to smithereens, nothing left."

"Alright, alright," said Breanne, "I get it."

My past life annihilated, just like that, she thought. *All my paintings destroyed and everything I had left of my parents. Damn it, are they still alive? Will I ever know for sure? Was my father really in that bomber? He did this to us, to me...*

"And what about Elsa?" she said, trying to salvage something from the wreckage of her dead heart.

"Remarkably, her house is intact, as is every second or third one in the street. We all played a round of nuclear Russian roulette. Not everyone made it."

None of us made it, thought Breanne.

"Now there's flame raining from the sky, fires breaking out in some of the remaining houses," said Jain. The car swerved. "And people running everywhere. Get out of the fucking way!"

Breanne could hear screams of distress and shouts of alarm, wails of grief and moans of pain. It was a symphony of despair, the plaintive notes of human suffering rising and falling like jarring, broken chords.

"Is there anything we can do to help?" she asked Jain.

"Fuck no. What are we meant to do? Go out there and burn to death too? Geez, there's some grisly scenes, people melting, others running around on fire." Jain gagged. "No water to be had to fight any of the blazes. I kind of envy the fact you're blind."

"Oh, I'm real lucky."

"You are compared to these poor sods."

"We need to check if Elsa's alright." Breanne fumbled to find the button to lower the door window. She pressed it, hot air rushing into the car.

"Get that damn window back up," Jain barked. "It's a fucking inferno out there."

Breanne kept the window down. "I think I can hear her." She called out the window, "Elsa. Elsa!"

"There's nothing we can do for her," said Jain, yet she slowed the car, perhaps in some type of unconscious sympathy.

"Breanne!" shrieked the old woman from somewhere nearby.

"It's her. It's Elsa. Stop the car," Breanne said to Jain, then through the window, "Over here, Elsa!"

The voice got louder, its pitch rising higher to a piercing scream. "Help me. Oh, God, it hurts!"

"We've got to get her out. She's probably trapped in her house."

Breanne fumbled around again, this time to find the door handle. She heard a click just before she found it, and when she tugged, it did nothing. Jain had locked the door remotely.

"Stay in the car, there's nothing you can do for her," Jain said, speeding up again. "We need to escape."

What escape is there now? thought Breanne, turning in her seat to look back blindly in what she guessed was the direction of Elsa's house. There a ghostly wisp resembling the old woman rose into the sky, consumed in fire. Elsa burned from the feet upwards, the old woman's face twisted in agony even in death. Her immolated soul joined with the legions of the dead ascending into the sky. They were converging on a single point—the monster. It blazed overhead like the awful eye of an all-seeing deity.

Breanne stared up at it, through the roof of the car, and saw the death of a world reflected in that baleful gaze.

47

"Oh my God," said Jain as she brought the car to a sharp halt, having revved hard to get up the steep driveway of Marc's parents' house.

"What?" asked Breanne, fighting with the still-locked door handle, desperate to get out, but even more desperate to escape from her debilitating blindness, sick of relying on Jain to describe everything.

"Oh my *God*," Jain repeated in shocked disbelief. The unlock mechanism clicked and she exited, saying, "No, please, no," over and over.

"What's happening?" asked Breanne, getting out of the car, but freezing on the spot as she realised she couldn't navigate by herself. She felt along the car's frame, taking tentative steps. "Ouch."

Both the car and the concrete driveway were scorching hot, and she fled from them, dancing about until she found a patch of grass, which was only a mild relief. She could smell singed lawn. It was an earthy, acrid stench. She felt its dry crackle under her shoes.

The atmosphere was oppressive, the air hot and close. She tried to take a deep breath but everywhere she turned there were wafting banks of pungent smoke which made Breanne choke and cough. Her raw skin was seared by the ambient heat of nearby fires, which cackled evilly as they burned. The sweat pouring off her made it even worse, like she was drowning, her skin suffocating in the mugginess.

"What the hell is happening?" she shouted, not sure where Jain was anymore. She could no longer hear her speaking. Breanne probed around with her feet, arms outstretched. She found a tree. It was on fire. It burnt her already blistered and agonised hands. She howled and danced on the spot, shaking her hands about. There was no relief from the pain, but she had to get a grip on herself. She swallowed hard, fighting down a panic attack.

If I was ever justified in having one, though, she thought, *now would be the time.*

But she didn't have that luxury. She was blind and lost in a burning hell-scape.

"Jain!" she screamed. "Where the fuck are you?"

"I'm here," came the reply, so close Breanne jumped.

"Fuck! You startled me. Let's go inside. I can barely breathe out here and I'm frightened."

"We can't," said Jain.

"Why?"

"The house is on fire."

48

They retreated to a rocky embankment behind the house which overlooked the village, the only place mildly free of burning trees and scrub. Jain helped Breanne to find a place on a patch of dirt and then sat down beside her.

"It's quite the sight," said Jain, her voice flat and numb, "all those houses going up in smoke, like a bonfire night but in the daytime."

Breanne was treated to a similar, yet distinct sight, the burning core of the monster and the immolated souls it gathered lighting up the darkness of her blind eyes. There were now so many it was impossible to make out individuals in the fiery mass.

"Amelia and Jacub?" she asked hoarsely, her throat dry from smoke.

"Nothing left of them but charred corpses," said Jain. She cried quietly.

Breanne reached out a hand to touch her shoulder, but instead Jain fell in under her armpit, hugged her tight. It was painful with her burned skin, yet the physical contact was exhilarating.

Maybe if I'm all she has left, then she'll have to love me?

"We got the laptop, but at what cost?" Jain asked between body-racking sobs. "We weren't here to save them."

"If we'd stayed we'd have burned as well," offered Breanne.

"At least we got the Jag out. Jacub would have appreciated that." Jain chuckled darkly. "I wonder whatever happened to Marc's miniature collection, back at our own place. He loved those miniatures, but he left them behind to save me, and to save this."

Jain tapped her fingers on something with a clicking sound. "Do you really think we can save Marc with just this laptop?"

I don't fucking know, it's your plan, thought Breanne.

"All we can do is try," she said soothingly.

"I'm not ready yet," said Jain, her voice filled with sorrow. "I don't know how to change any of this. And we don't know how much battery this thing has left. We sure as shit aren't going to be able to recharge it any time soon. Plus, I've got to build us some type of shelter. Maybe there's a tent in the pool shed."

"There's a pool shed?"

"Yeah, a little tin one where Marc's parents stored their miscellaneous junk and pool supplies."

"Did it burn?"

"No."

"Then why don't we live in it?"

Jain laughed with a single exclamation. "My brain must not be working anymore. I'll go check it out."

"Come right back."

"I will."

And she did.

"The shed's out," said Jain. "It's hotter than Hades in there. The metal walls are scorching to the touch. I could barely breathe going in there. But I did find some useful stuff—steel and canvas cots, some sleeping bags, and this tent."

"Any water?"

"The mother lode. Marc's parents hoarded the stuff in these old plastic cranberry juice bottles, though they're a bit warped from the heat. Crazy thing about Marc's parents, they had a leak in their water pipes, so they didn't have running water turned on all the time and—"

"Give me a drink, I'm dying," croaked Breanne.

"Don't be stupid, you're not dying." Jain took a sloshing gulp from the bottle and then held it to Breanne's cracked, peeling lips.

"It hurts to drink," said Breanne. "It even burns in my throat and stomach."

"Do you think you've got radiation sickness?"

"We both do, don't we, being out here in the fallout? I'm just worse because I'm also burnt like a supermarket BBQ chicken."

"Remember the way the skin on those things looked, all greasy and brown, with charred black bits?"

"Oh, thanks," Breanne said sarcastically.

"You don't look *that* bad, though," said Jain, trying to recover and failing, the placating tone obvious.

"I used to work in a chicken takeaway place," said Breanne, leaning into the situation with grim humour. "And I had to get inside these big ovens, clean them out after they'd cooked a batch of rotisserie chickens."

"Gross."

"Yeah, it was. The way they'd shed their fat, turned to liquid. I called it the Chicken Holocaust."

"Grim."

Breanne's laughter was like a croaking toad. "We're the chickens, Jain. We're cooking in the heat of that damned monster as its fire rages up in the sky."

"It's starting to pass over now, getting further away as the sun heads off to the west. It stirred up the fallout clouds a bit, but they're hanging around."

"And we can't escape the fallout."

They sat in silence for a while, the sound of screaming in the distance mingling with the crackle and roar of fires.

"Maybe we can think of something, you know, to take care of the fallout as well, put it in the book on the laptop?" said Jain.

Breanne closed her blind eyes, exhausted. "I don't know if I have the imagination for it."

"That's the whole reason I brought you on this quest, isn't it?"

"More fool you," said Breanne, thinking the situation was hopeless if it all depended on her. She felt the thread of her life fraying with each passing hour.

"Okay, so we need to deal with the fallout, and the monster, and save Marc," said Jain. "I'll make a list. I love lists. You can conquer anything if you make a list, tick off one thing at a time."

"It's going to take a special idea to do all that."

"Lucky you're a special girl."

Girl? She thinks I'm just a kid, thought Breanne.

"I'm a woman," she said, driving a stake in the sand of her self-esteem.

"Of course you are."

"I like you."

"Thanks, Breanne. I like you too."

"But you love Marc." Breanne tried to say it without sounding pouty and defensive, but failed. In doing so, though, she got her point across.

"Of course I love Marc," she said, driving her own stake in the sand, and, as a result, through Breanne's heart. "Don't be jealous. You and I have been through a lot. I know I give you a hard time, but you're my best friend... my *only* friend now."

"You're the only friend I've ever had," said Breanne.

The problem is you're the one person I don't want to be just a friend.

49

That night was a bad one. It was cold, yet Breanne's body went through terrible hot flushes, the burns covering her skin weeping puss, which then cooled, making her shiver. Jain did her best to make her comfortable, but she had so little. There was no means to boil water. The antibiotics and painkillers had been lost in the house fire. And what bedding they had clung to Breanne's skin painfully. Then there was Jain's own wound, which she suffered without complaint, though with the occasional hiss and wince of pain and discomfort when she shifted her leg.

"Let me die," wheezed Breanne shallowly, her lungs feeling like they were made of thin, torn tissue paper, unable to pump enough air.

"It'll be dawn soon," said Jain reassuringly. "The sun makes everything seem a little better."

Breanne soon disabused her of this. "And with it comes the monster. I can see it in my mind." She closed her eyelids, the eyeballs beneath flickering like during REM sleep. "It's orbiting the world, shadowing its prey like a patient hunter, gathering its strength, waiting to pounce. All the while it rains fire, killing en masse, harvesting souls and wrapping itself up in their protective fabric, making ready."

"For the transformation you mentioned?"

Breanne spoke in the flat monotone of a psychic channel receiving a message from beyond the veil. "It will be a vast moth, terrible in its beauty, its wings to span a continent. Its shadow is death, a dark blade to sever us from our life force. It seeks to swallow us, recycle our energy. Humanity means nothing to it. All that matters is that it defeats the Anathema, frees the

Earth from the bonds of the shining source of this false light."

"False light?"

"The sun," said Breanne in an eerie whisper.

"The sun gives us everything though. Light, heat, makes the crops grow. It's the source of life."

"Of human life, yes, but the monster is born of the Earth, and the Earth tires of us. We're parasites to it, sucking its blood and feeding it to its foe. It would see us dead."

"The Earth is trying to kill us?" Jain sounded incredulous.

"We are the children of the Anathema. We are the shadows of the true form, copies of a purer template. Only with the false light do we cast our silhouettes into this reality."

"And what is the true form?"

"The monster," said Breanne in hushed awe.

"The monster is an abomination."

"No, it is the perfect creature, eternal yet finite. Its symbol is the ring. It is the snake eating its own tail, consuming itself as it is born."

"The ouroboros?"

"Yes, it is that which the Anathema is jealous of, tries to copy with its endless circling of the Earth. In doing so, it has become a noose around the neck of the planet. The Earth wants to cast it off."

Breanne opened her eyes but saw less for it.

"We cannot stop this," she said. "It is destiny."

50

"I don't believe you," said Jain, shaking Breanne by the shoulders.

"You're hurting me," said Breanne, the jolts of agony shooting through her body like electric shocks.

"I don't care, you're wrong. I can save Marc."

"All you can do is place yourself in line with fate."

"We've got the laptop, though, we've got the book!"

"It is already written."

"No, it can be changed. What are you saying? You were meant to help me come up with another ending."

"We can alter the content of the conflict but not the conclusion. Everything is a cycle. Jain, I can feel my soul shaking itself loose. Please, before I go…"

"No, not yet, don't leave me. I need you," Jain pleaded. "Look, we'll write the book, right now, before the sun comes up, before the monster returns."

Breanne heard the sound of the laptop booting up.

"I'm praying there's some battery left in this thing," said Jain, tapping the keys impatiently, coaxing the computer back to life. "Come on, come on."

Breanne laughed.

"And what's so funny?" asked Jain.

"You'll see."

There was more tapping of keys and clicking of the touchpad. "I've found the file," said Jain. "It was the last one accessed. It's called *Kaiju Sunrise*."

"Fitting, I suppose. It's coming."

"The sunrise? Yeah, it is."

"I meant the monster."

"I'll look."

Breanne heard Jain shuffling around, the tent flaps swishing open.

"Okay, that thing is fucking nuts," said Jain.

"I can see it," said Breanne, closing her eyes once more to get a better view.

"It's like a giant glowing spaceship or something."

"It's a cocoon, the Kaiju's chrysalis."

"It's huge, nearly as big as the sun, at least lengthways. It's long like a tube."

"If only we were so perfect," Breanne said in awe. The fear of her impending death had left her. Now she wished only to witness the inevitable and then be free of all this, free of her desires, of the burden she carried.

"The sun will love me even if you can't," she said to Jain.

"What?" Jain said absently, distracted as she fiddled with the computer. "There's not a lot of battery. We don't have much time."

"True," said Breanne, lying on her back, watching the chrysalis glide across her second sight like a shape seen in a lazy, drifting cloud.

"Okay, I've got the file open. I'm reading…"

Breanne smiled, waiting for the inevitable. Long minutes passed.

"Holy fuck!" said Jain.

"Hmm?" said Breanne placidly, feeling her life force drifting like the chrysalis, only tenuously anchored to the Earth now.

"It's all here. The whole fucking story!"

Breanne chuckled.

"Is this what you were laughing about?" snapped Jain. "Like this is all some cruel joke to you?"

"A joke played on all of us," said Breanne.

"I'm not laughing. It's laid out in exact detail, not just what Marc wrote, but everything that happened afterwards to Marc and I, and then to you."

"I told you, it is written."

More time passed as Jain kept reading.

"Oh my God, Breanne," she said, "you're fucking obsessed with me!"

It doesn't seem to matter anymore, thought Breanne.

"You thought you could trick me into choosing you over Marc?" said Jain, jabbing a bony finger hard into Breanne's raw skin. There wasn't any more pain to feel. In Breanne's mind, the chrysalis throbbed.

"Well? Answer me, you fucking psycho," hissed Jain. When she got no reply, Jain started typing, the keys chattering like rattling bones. "I'll show you, Breanne. I'll make sure you never get between me and Marc."

Breanne smiled wanly as Jain killed her off.

51

Dying didn't bother Breanne. It was a relief—the burns, the radiation sickness, her desires and needs, it was all too much to carry. She left behind the heavy physical body, with all its demands and restrictions, and floated away. All that concerned her now was freedom, and that meant avoiding the monster and its hunger for souls. She didn't want to come between Marc and Jain anymore. She didn't want Jain for herself. In fact, she wanted nothing, because to want meant becoming trapped in that chrysalis and being used to perpetuate the cycle of death and rebirth.

Marc and Jain can have each other, she thought, for she was no longer able to speak. *They have their fate. I have mine.*

But there was one last thing to do before she left this plane. She had to watch the ending Jain made for herself, or at least thought she made for herself, writing on the computer, guided by a power greater than any human mind.

As Breanne's soul ascended into the sky it passed close to the chrysalis, which loomed over her like a black sun, casting its dread shadow across the Earth. Military planes swarmed around its bloated husk like swarms of flies, a mere impotent annoyance to the gargantuan, blimp-like cocoon.

What happened next was inevitable, though it contained one stroke of creative genius by Jain. In her frantic typing on the computer, impatient for a solution to her desperate conundrum, she accidentally stumbled on a nexus point of fate, a way to impact events.

She sped up the timeline.

The chrysalis cracked open, splitting like an elongated egg. Breanne's soul recoiled from it, sensing the horrifying presence which waited inside, ravenous from its slumber, all those millions of human souls already consumed to fuel its transformation.

In the burning crucible of the chrysalis, the monster had taken on its new form. It was the God moth she'd seen in her waking nightmares.

Mothzen.

The creature was weak from the change, which had been forced on it too quickly. But it was angry and driven by a dread instinct to consume. Now it came forth to feed.

And it hungered for the power of a star.

52

Breanne could see the light of the true sun reflected in the bulbous, multifaceted compound eyes which poked their way free of the cocoon's husk first. They sparkled like disco balls, blinding in their terrifying majesty, beams of light scattered in all directions and in all colours. They were a kaleidoscopic nightmare, revealing the awful intelligence of the beast as it shifted and fought its way out of the chrysalis.

The hole in this fleshy shell widened, and antennae unfurled like barbed whips, lashing the air, feeling for prey, sensing Breanne's presence. Furry mandibles chomped away the dead flesh of the cocoon, gnashing like the whirring blades of a thresher, keen to harvest her energy.

Goaded by a terror so total it transcended any sensations of the body, Breanne struggled—not for life, which was already lost to her—but for the right to be dissolved by oblivion, to escape into the void of space.

I don't want to burn in the fiery core of the monster for all eternity. I've suffered enough. I deserve silence.

As it emerged more fully, Mothzen's body swelled, the furry dark hair of its abdomen ruffling and going stiff with aggressive intent, emanating violence. The mandibles clashed together around a cavernous mouth, dripping with thick, rainbow saliva. The strings of slavering drool glistened in the light which shone from deep inside, emanating from the monster's burning heart. Breanne saw that fiery light and knew that in it there awaited a fate worse than death.

Her ghostly form quivered violently as Mothzen drew in a massive breath, tasting the radioactive fallout. The powerful current of air sucked at her, and she fought against it, swimming against an invisible flow. She knew if she went inside that hungry, gaping hole, and was swallowed by Mothzen, she would be trapped, digested, dissolved into her constituent parts, and fed into the furnace which powered the monster. There was true hell, where she would be forced to relive the suffering of existence, over and over. She would be reborn, repeating the cycle of pain and death, instead of being released from ouroboros' noose.

Breanne hovered over the ravenous mouth, her fate hanging by a thread as she was drawn inside, the mandibles gnashing the air in furious hunger.

She was saved at the last moment by Jain.

Breanne could feel the guilt of the woman who had signed her death warrant, and Jain did what she could to allow her to escape. She distracted the monster with the furious buzzing attacks of the military planes, wielding them clumsily with her writing. Shooting upwards, through and amongst their formations, Breanne sensed a familiar presence in one of those planes. She turned to it, saw his face. Here was the last bond tying her to this existence. She decided to cut the noose from around her neck, the one which had held her in thrall her entire life.

I know you did what you thought was right. And for that, I forgive you, Dad, she thought.

Free of this last burden, her soul shot up, past the crumbling chrysalis, discarded by the monster and falling to Earth like a humongous parachute catching the wind. It drifted away to land in the ocean, there to be devoured by shoals of hungry fish, nibbling at its massive bulk in their thousands.

Onwards Breanne climbed, Mothzen thrashing angrily at the suffocating swarm of planes. They fought in an oil slick patina of swirling toxic fallout, the rainbow clouds reflected in the beautiful shifting patterns of the monster as it unfurled its colossal wings with a cracking snap which cut the air like a sonic boom.

The hurricane winds it generated sent planes spiralling from the sky, crashing to the ground in explosive blossoms of fiery red and yellow flowers. Others were skimmed over the horizon like stones tossed across a lake. Few managed to stay airborne, limping away from the fight heavily damaged.

Breanne found she didn't care if her father was among these meagre survivors. Such things were far beneath her now, as was Jain and her attempts to save herself and reunite with Marc, though Breanne was witness to the results of her improvised plan.

With a second, mighty flap of its stunningly patterned wings, Mothzen scattered the radiation-laden clouds, sending them far from Australia's skies. But in doing so, Breanne saw that Jain doomed the world, the toxic fallout spreading to cover all the nations and oceans of the Earth. With this desperate act a time bomb started ticking, the end of human life inevitable.

Then Jain did what Breanne knew she would, what she must do. Driven by her desperate need to free Marc, she gave Mothzen what it most desired. With a squealing cry of ecstatic joy, the monster flew at the sun. But the confrontation had come too soon for Mothzen, its power not yet recovered in full.

This was the gamble Jain had staked everything on.

The battle was short-lived. A mere baby, newly reborn, Mothzen was no match for the Anathema. With a shrill ultrasonic shriek of pain, the monster was consumed by the immolating tendrils of the sun's fiery corona.

Breanne saw Jain surge from the tent, fists pumping the air with exhilaration at her triumph. But her celebration was premature, her victory Pyrrhic. From her vantage point, high above, Breanne got a glimpse of the tragic consequences of Jain's plan.

In one way she was successful. Mothzen's corporeal body burned up in a colossal puff of disintegrating embers and rainbow smoke. But in her ignorance Jain had also doomed Marc even further. His prison—the monster's blazing heart—remained intact.

Free of its fleshy encumbrance, this second sun tumbled from the sky, arcing into the Pacific Ocean like a falling meteorite. It struck with the power of a detonating atomic bomb, throwing forth a great circular wave which rippled across the face of the ocean, devastating distant coastlines. The water hissed furiously at the impact site, a towering pillar of steam rising to obscure the burning ball as it sank into the depths, there to fester like a sore and one day return.

Feeling detached from this development, Breanne took one last look at life and turned her back on it. She floated up into space, escaping the bonds of Earth, dissolving forever in the vast void of nothingness beyond.

The End

www.ingramcontent.com/pod-product-compliance
Lightning Source LLC
Chambersburg PA
CBHW061242170626
46809CB00007B/2783